P9-EDV-906

MEDUSA ISLAND

Stuart & Linda Macfarlane

DISCARDED

©2008 Nartea Publishing
a Div. of DNA Press, LLC

MEDUSA ISLAND

©Copyright by Stuart and Linda Macfarlane

©2008 by Nartea Publishing, a Div. of DNA Press, LLC. All rights reserved.

All rights reserved under International and Pan-American Copyright conventions. No part of this book may be reproduced or transmitted in any form or by any means, electronic or mechanical, including photocopying, recording, or any information storage and retrieval system, without permission in writing to DNA Press at the address posted at www.dnapress.com. Published in the United States by Nartea Publishing, a division of DNA Press, LLC.

Library of Congress Cataloging-in-Publication Data
Macfarlane, Stuart. Medusa Island / Stuart & Linda Macfarlane. — 1st ed.
    p. cm.
Summary: Twelve-year-olds Simon and Ross meet snake-haired Melissa and join her in trying to save her island home and its inhabitants from the mad scientist who has used a blend of ancient magic and modern science to alter DNA and create mythological creatures.

ISBN 978-1-933255-45-3 (alk. paper)

[1. Animals, Mythical—Fiction. 2. Imaginary creatures—Fiction. 3. Genetic engineering—Fiction. 4. Magic—Fiction. 5. Adventure and adventurers—Fiction. 6. Science fiction. 7. Humorous stories.]
I.Macfarlane, Linda. II. Title.

    PZ7.M1666Med 2008
    [Fic]—dc22

    2008001917

DNA Press, LLC
www.dnapress.com
editors@dnapress.com

Publisher: Nartea Publishing, a Div. of DNA Press, LLC
Executive Editor: Alexander Kuklin
Art Direction: Alex Nartea
Cover Art: Nei Ruffino
Vignettes by Drawizart

TABLE OF CONTENTS

*This book is dedicated to all good people who battle fearlessly
against "mad scientists that want to rule the world".*

*Thanks to Joseph and Emilie Conroy of Stone Bench Associates
Literary Agency for all their help and support.*

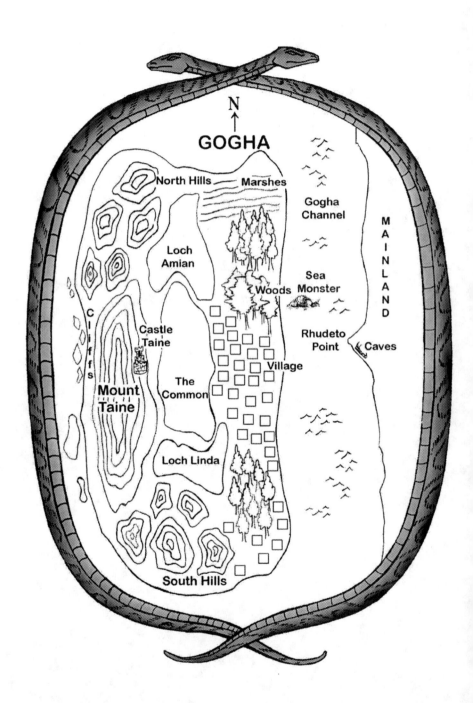

CHAPTER 1
In which Chris disappears or Simon discovers that he has lost his marbles

S imon was the first to arrive at the clubhouse. He checked his Ultra-Accurate-Atomic-Wrist-Watch—16:59:59 precisely. Simon was very particular about time and hated wasting even a microsecond. "Look after the seconds and the hours will look after themselves," he often said—much to the annoyance of his friends.

When Ross arrived at 17:01:42 Simon greeted him with a punch on the arm.

"You're late," he snapped.

"I'm not," insisted Ross.

"Are."

"Not."

"At least you're not as late as Chris," said Simon.

"Who?"

"Chris."

"Who's Chris?"

"Don't make me angry," said Simon.

"You're already angry, Stupid," sneered Ross.

"Not."

"Are."

"I'm not," yelled Simon, swinging a punch at Ross.

"Missed," said Ross, wiping blood from his nose.

"Yeah right."

"So who's Chris?" asked Ross, kicking his best friend.

"What do you mean who's Chris?" said Simon, punching Ross in the stomach.

"I don't know anyone called Chris," said Ross, karate chopping Simon's arm.

"He's the person who's five minutes and thirty three seconds late," said Simon looking at his Ultra-Accurate-Atomic-Wrist-Watch. "Come on, let's find him. We're going to be late for the movies if we don't get moving."

"But I keep telling you," said Ross, "I don't know anyone called Chris."

"Don't start that again or I'll give you another black eye to match the two you've already got."

"You and whose army?" said Ross—ducking.

Under protest, Ross followed Simon to the house where he claimed Chris lived. The door was answered by Brutus. Brutus was two years older than Simon and Ross yet, although only fourteen, he was already six foot three. He was a kind gentle boy who was often misunderstood. In fact many thought he was a cruel bully—especially those people he regularly beat up.

Simon looked Brutus up and down—he was built like a truck.

"You still work out fighting polar bears?" asked Simon.

"Don't be ridiculous," growled Brutus. "I haven't done that since I got banned from the zoo."

"That's a shame," said Simon, "but I guess beating up the younger kids keeps you in shape."

"Look, what do you want, Tik-Tok?" snarled Brutus.

"I'm looking for Chris."

"Who?"

"Chris," said Simon, beginning to wonder if he was the subject of some nasty April Fool's prank even though it was mid July, "your brother."

"You're starting to annoy me?" said Brutus stepping forward

and towering over Simon in the way a volcano towers over a little village just before destroying it with molten lava. 'I don't have a brother, I never have had a brother and I never will have a brother."

As Brutus slowly, for although he was gigantic in the tallness department he was sadly dwarfish in the brains department, tried to decide whether to break one of Simon's arms or perhaps snap one of his legs, Ross grabbed his friend by the t-shirt.

"Let's get out of here," he yelled, dragging Simon away, saving him from a painful stay in hospital.

Simon and Ross arrived at the movies eight minutes and twenty seconds after the movie had started. Normally Simon would have been furious but this had been a far from normal evening so being eight minutes and twenty seconds late was the least of his worries. He didn't watch any of the movie, instead he sat lost in thought. This morning he had two best friends. Now he only had one. Yet nobody seemed to have noticed that Chris had vanished from the face of the earth—or even remembered that just a few hours earlier he'd been flunking his history exam. This was worrying, very worrying.

After the movie, Simon hurried home, to speak to his mother about Chris. His mom, Mrs. Wanabea Fairleywelthy, didn't hear him come in. Simon watched her lying curled up on her pink-leather sofa scoffing chocolates by the handful. He loved his mother and wouldn't swap her for the whole universe. But there were a few things about her he'd like to change. Recently he'd made a list of everything that irritated him—but he'd got bored when he reached number eighty-four. Third on his list was the fact that she never, ever left her pink-leather sofa. Over the years he'd seen her eat, sleep, swim, dance, cook, paraglide, and do many other things on her pink-leather sofa. He remembered with embarrassment the time she'd taken it to the amusement park. Simon had helped carry it onto the Big-Dipper, Shockwave and all the other roller coaster rides. Second on his list was her bedraggled appearance—her hair hadn't been cut since she was a child and she wore it in a huge bun, perched on top of her head like a dead hedgehog. But absolutely, definitely at the very top of Simon's 'most annoying things about mom' list, was that a week ago she'd confiscated his cell phone. Simon and Ross had been having a competition to see how many different countries they could contact. When their parents received massive bills the boys were banned from using any phone for six months. Simon found this particularly annoying as the score was standing at ninety-nine counties each and he desperately wanted to be first to reach the winning target of one-hundred.

"Mom, can Chris come for dinner tomorrow?" asked Simon.

"That would be nice," replied Mom.

"Will you make his favorite pudding?"

"That would be nice," replied Mom.

"Then can we go on a spaceship to Mars?"

"That would be nice," replied Mom.

Just as he thought, his mother was too busy watching her favorite TV soaps to listen. Simon grabbed the remotes and the three televisions fizzled out of life.

"Mom! Listen to me! This is important!" he yelled.

"I am listening honey," replied Mom, turning the page of her magazine. "Remind me what you said."

"My friend Chris has disappeared," blurted Simon.

"Oh that's a shame," said Mom, filling in the answer to Five Down on the crossword puzzle. "Never mind he'll probably feel better by morning."

"So you remember Chris?" quizzed Simon.

"Of course. Now let me think . . . is he the nice boy with the spotty face?"

"No Mom that's Ross."

"Oh . . . is he the horrid boy with the nice face?"

"No Mom."

"Well then . . . what about the quite nice boy with the not so horrid face?"

"Mom! Chris was here last night. Remember?"

"Last night . . . mmmm . . ." said Mom, pensively and annoyingly slowly. "Did we have boiled cabbage for dinner last night?"

"Oh forget it," said Simon, exasperated. "I'm going to bed."

Simon lay deep in thought. "Either I'm going crazy or everyone else is, and, as there's less chance of everyone else going crazy all at the same time, it must be me." This was a very unpleasant thought. Then he had another thought. Not a thought that was more pleasant—just a different thought. He remembered the photo he'd taken of Chris and Ross at the zoo a few days earlier. He jumped out of bed and yanked open his bedside cabinet. There it was lying safely under a pile of used tissues and bits of bubble gum that, although well chewed, hadn't completely lost their flavor. Simon snatched up the photo. To his great relief Chris was there. He wasn't going crazy. Now he had proof that his friend really did exist.

But, as Simon stared in disbelief, the photo began to change.

"No!" cried Simon. "Oh no!"

The image of Chris faded. Within a few seconds only Ross and the three monkeys remained. Chris was gone!

CHAPTER 2
In which two more people disappear or Simon discovers that he has lost three times as many marbles as he first thought

A t precisely 06:58:00 the cuckoo clock cuckooed to inform Simon that it was time to get up. At the same time Simon's Ultra-Accurate-Atomic-Wrist-Watch buzzed, five alarm clocks rang, and the radio blasted out some 'good morning' music.

But for Simon this was not a good morning and at 07:02:42 he was still in bed. This was most unusual for he hated wasting even a microsecond. Eventually, at 07:04:03, Simon forced himself to get up. The only reason he bothered was because he had a science lesson. Today, Mr. Nutronbom would demonstrate what happens when oxygen and hydrogen are combined and exposed to a naked flame. There was every chance that he'd blow up the entire school and Simon wasn't going to miss that for the world.

After breakfast Simon met up with Ross and they walked to school. On the way they talked about girls, in particular about the new girl, Ann Dromeda, whom they both really, really liked a lot. They talked about football. They even talked about politics— though only to say "let's not talk about politics". The only thing they didn't talk about (apart from not really having an in-depth discussion on politics and, to be completely mathematically correct, an infinite number of other things) was Chris. Simon avoided the subject for he didn't want his friend to think that he was crazy— even though he was now convinced that he was.

The first lesson was history and the first thing their teacher, Miss Teryee, did was call the roll. Simon hated this; she called the same names every single day. It was such a waste of time. And although he hated history he hated wasting time more than any thing.

"Carol Singer," called out Miss Teryee.

"Present Miss Teryee," trilled Carol.

"Graeme Sweeney," called Miss Teryee.

Silence.

"Graeme."

More silence.

"Graeme Sweeney!" bellowed Miss Teryee. "Wake up!"

"Oh . . . here ma'am," said Graeme, adjusting his pillow, "I wasn't sleeeee . . . zzzz . . . ZZZZ."

"Justin Tyme," called Miss Teryee.

"Yep, I'm definitely here ma'am," muttered Justin as Miss Teryee was about to mark him absent.

"Ann Dromeda," continued Miss Teryee.

"Here ma'am," said Ann sweetly.

When the roll had been taken, Simon nudged Ross hard in the ribs.

"She didn't call Jack Rabbet or Mary Queen—and they're not in class," he gasped.

"What are you talking about?" scowled Ross.

"Jack and Mary . . . Miss Teryee didn't call out their names. And they didn't say 'absent' because they're not here to say anything. And if they're not here and if Miss Teryee didn't call their names, that means that they must have vanished just like Chris," blurted out Simon, not making a lot of sense.

Ross stared at his friend as if to say, 'You're crazy.'

"You're crazy," he said rather loudly.

"Silence," bellowed Miss Tyree. "I will not have anyone talking in my class . . . apart for me of course, or if I specifically ask someone a question that requires an answer or if there is an emergency situation in which remaining silent would be adverse to the safety of fellow pupils or if there is a nuclear explosion or . . ."

Simon remained silent for the rest of the lesson. In fact he hardly said a word all day—not even when Mr. Nutronbom almost blew up the entire school (but didn't). Instead of talking, Simon thought. He thought and he thought and he thought. In fact he thought so much his brain very nearly went numb with the effort. First he thought about going crazy. Was being crazy really just like being normal except that your friends disappear? And, he thought, 'if I am crazy will everybody in the whole world eventually disappear?' For a short while he thought about Ann. He wondered if she'd be the girlfriend of someone who was crazy. He wondered if she'd disappear before he got the chance to tell her that he loved her. He wondered if he'd still love her after she disappeared—for he expected this was the sort of thing that crazy people did.

Simon had Double-Cheese-Burger with French-Fries for lunch. Possibly this nutritional food helped stimulate his brain for, in the afternoon, his thoughts were much more creative. He worked out a way of proving whether he really was crazy or his friends were just disappearing.

"I need your help," he said to Ross on the way home, "to break into school."

"Have you completely lost your marbles?" gasped Ross as he fumbled in his schoolbag for his asthma inhaler.

"Hopefully not . . . but I need to break into school to find out."

"Why?"

"I can't explain now but trust me, I need to do this," said Simon. "Are you in?"

"Okay," replied Ross reluctantly.

"Good. Meet me at the school gate at precisely 21:00."

"Right."

"And come in disguise," added Simon, "in case anyone spots us."

And so the plan was set. Soon Simon would find out whether he was going crazy or people were mysteriously disappearing . . . or neither . . . or both.

CHAPTER 3
Simon breaks into school and finds out that he's not crazy but makes his mom crazy

S imon stole through the streets hugging the shadows to avoid being noticed. Since there was no one around at the time, this was particularly pointless, but he did so anyway. He reached School Avenue without being seen by anyone except two cats and a dog but they promised not to tell. Nearing the school he spotted someone standing at the gates. Simon hid behind a lamppost and watched. A clown, complete with a big red painted smile and glowing cheeks was rocking back and forward in size twenty-two clogs.

"Drat," hissed Simon, kicking the lamppost, "all my plans ruined by a stupid clown."

But he quickly realized that it wasn't a proper clown. It was Ross dressed as a clown.

"Why are you dressed like that you twit?" said Simon.

"You said come in disguise," grunted Ross.

"I said in disguise—not fancy dress!" said Simon. "You should have dressed like me."

Ross looked his friend up and down. He was wearing his father's duffle-coat, which was so long it swept the ground. The sleeves made Simon look as if he had no hands. Around his neck was a luminous pink scarf and on his head a bright yellow and green tartan cap.

"You look more like a clown than I do," sneered Ross.

"Come on," said Simon. "We don't have time to argue—

we've got a school to break into."

Breaking in was amazingly simple, especially since Simon had had the foresight to leave a window open in the science lab. Getting through the window was the difficult bit. Ross's clown outfit was heavily padded and it took a huge amount of pushing and shoving to force him through. Simon's long coat made climbing in tricky but eventually both boys were inside and stumbling along the corridors towards the history room. There on Miss Teryee's desk was the register.

Simon picked it up cautiously as though it held a great secret. His heart impersonated a drum as slowly and carefully he scanned the names.

"Yes!" he cheered, as if he'd scored a penalty in the cup final. "Between Luke Owette and Liza Storrie there's a blank space where Jack Rabbet's name used to be. And there are spaces where Chris and Mary's names once were."

"Mmmm," said Ross pensively. "Okay, so there are three blank lines and that's odd but how could three people possibly disappear without a trace and why would you remember them when no one else does?"

"Maybe because of my superior intelligence," said Simon.

"No," replied Ross, "More likely because you're so obsessed with detail that you even notice how much the grass has grown overnight."

Simon resented that remark—it had been weeks since he last measured the grass in his garden—and anyway that had been an experiment. He clenched his fists to punch Ross but changed his mind.

"Something weird is going on and we need to stop it before everyone disappears," he said.

Ross's reply was drowned by the sound of sirens and the squeal of brakes as four police cars sped into the school playground.

"Let's get out of here," yelled Simon.

Tripping over each other, the boys hurried towards the science lab. From the other end of the corridor a commanding voice bellowed, "Stop or we shoot to kill."

The boys stopped.

"We can't shoot them," said a second voice, "We don't have guns."

"I know that you idiot," said the first voice, "but they don't."

"Oh," said the second voice.

The boys began running.

"Freeze," yelled the second voice, "We have nuclear missiles and we're not afraid to use them."

The boys kept running. They reached the science lab. All they had to do was get through the open window and they'd be safe. Ross clambered onto a desk and squeezed his head and arms through. He wriggled and twisted until half his body was hanging out. But the huge padding around his stomach got stuck. He kept wriggling but the harder he tried the more stuck he became.

"Hurry up," yelled Simon.

"I can't move," said Ross.

"You're useless," snarled Simon.

Simon grabbed Ross's legs and pushed. But he wouldn't budge.

"You'll need to come back in and take off that stupid costume," yelled Simon.

Simon yanked on Ross's legs. Nothing. He yanked harder. With a ripping sound the costume tore free of the window. Ross flew back into the room, landing on top of Simon. They tumbled to the floor in a heap. The desk wobbled then crashed down on top of them. At that precise moment one of the police officers burst into the room.

"It's a couple of clowns," he called to his colleague.

"Just one clown," said Simon, indignantly, "I'm not dressed as a clown."

"You look more like a clown than your friend," said the officer.

"Told you," jeered Ross.

The boys were driven, at high speed, to the local police station and bundled into a tiny cell. Minutes later Ross's parents rushed in. They were extremely annoyed at their son for getting into trouble and said so. "We are extremely annoyed at our son for getting into trouble," they said to no one in particular.

An hour later, after an exceptionally mediocre episode of 'Hospital Holidays' had finished, Simon's mother reluctantly turned up—carried in on her pink-leather sofa by two police officers. She was extremely annoyed at having to miss her sixty-ninth favorite TV Soap, 'Young and Rustless'. At the same time Simon's dad arrived from his evening job as assistant fish gutter at the Ritzzz Hotel. He was wearing his best black suit with a black bow tie and had a Colt-45 strapped around his waist. Not having had time to wash, he smelt like week old road-kill. Fish eyes and tails stuck in his hair and fish guts dripped from his ears.

The boys and their parents were taken to the office of the Chief of Police. Simon and Ross were made to stand in front of the Chief's huge oak desk while their parents sat on Mrs. Fairleywelthy's pink-leather sofa at the back of the room. The Chief of Police rocked gently back and forward on his life-size wooden rocking horse. He was a stern man and you could tell that he hated children by the 'I Hate Children' badge he wore on his jacket.

"Burning down the town hall is a very serious matter," said the Chief of Police glowering at the boys.

"We didn't burn down the town hall," blurted out Ross. "We only broke into the school."

"Don't contradict me when I'm wrong," bellowed the Chief,

rocking more fiercely on his rocking horse, "and breaking into school without written permission from the Council is a very serious crime indeed."

"We had a good reason for breaking in sir," said Simon.

"Silence!" growled the Chief. "Don't you know that it's bad manners to speak before the age of eighteen?"

"The problem with kids these days is they don't watch enough telly," said Simon's mom in their defense. "In our day we were too busy watching telly to have time for silly things like breaking into schools and burning down town halls."

"We didn't burn down . . ." began Simon.

"Don't talk back to your mother," interrupted Simon's dad, though, as he was sucking on a cod head at the time, it sounded more like, "Gnnowntt tawwek kack doo goooor gugger."

"These children are completely out of control. I've a good mind to lock them up and throw away the key," growled the Chief. "But I can't!"

"Against the rules?" asked Ross's dad.

"No, all our locks are digital. They don't have keys. They have touch-pads."

"You could always write down the password and throw that away," suggested Ross's mom helpfully.

"Sadly petty bureaucracy limits the punishment I can give," moaned the Chief. "Having them hung, drawn and quartered would be my choice but all I can do is suspend them from school for a week."

The boys glanced at each other, struggling to hide their emotions. Being suspended from school for five days brought shame and humiliation on their families. But it could have been worse—they might have been suspended for just two days.

"Yippeeeee!" thought the boys—but remained respectably silent.

CHAPTER 4
Simon and Ross go fishing and are reunited with some stony cold friends

Monday morning was the first day of the boys' extra 'vacation'. As usual, Simon's first job was making his mother's breakfast. He prepared everything as quickly as he could and carried it on a huge silver tray; eight scrambled ostrich eggs, twelve slices of extra fatty bacon, five tins of baked beans, eleven monster sized burgers, nine fried daffodils and twenty-three slices of toast.

"Get out of the way What's-Your-Name, you're blocking the telly," his mom yelled appreciatively as he sat the breakfast on the table in front of her.

Simon's father was out on one of his part-time jobs. As well as being assistant fish gutter at the Ritzzz Hotel he drove a taxi during the nights and, at weekends, worked as a guide-dog for poor blind people who couldn't afford real dogs. All of this extra work supplemented the meager income from his main job as Mafia Hit Man and helped keep Mrs. Fairleywelthy in the comfort she'd insisted on becoming accustomed to.

With his father out working so much and his mother unwilling to leave her pink-leather sofa, Simon had to do most of the house-work. He never complained but it did annoy him that it wasted so much of his time. He was fanatically obsessive about time, space, cleanliness and most other things but apart from that he was a fairly happy go lucky boy. Simon was not clever but not stupid, not big but not small, not ugly but not stunningly handsome, not blue eyed but not yellow eyed. If fact in every way he was completely average—probably the most average boy on the planet.

After washing the breakfast dishes, Simon made his mom an after breakfast snack then grabbed his fishing gear and set out to meet Ross. The boys headed to their favorite fishing spot at Rhudeto Point. Here the rocks jutted out into the sea giving spectacular views up and down the coastline and across the water to the little island of Gogha half a mile away. The Point was an excellent fishing ground and the boys caught many large cod and haddock there. On one occasion Ross even landed a massive lobster but it grabbed his nose in its claws and he had to be rushed to hospital to have it removed (the lobster not the nose).

Although it was just ten o'clock, the sun was already beating down fiercely. The boys wore mirrored sunglasses and, as they scrambled across the rocks, little beams of reflected sunlight danced upon the waves. They attached juicy worms to their hooks and cast their lines, each eager to be first to catch a fish. But the fish had other plans and refused to play.

"We've been fishing for sixteen minutes and six seconds," said Simon after they'd been fishing for sixteen minutes and six seconds, "and we haven't even caught a sardine."

"Hardly surprising, Stupid," said Ross shaking his head. "There's no sardines within a hundred miles of here."

"You know what I mean."

"Be patient, a huge shoal could come along at any minute."

"I don't have time to be patient," said Simon. "Time is in short supply."

"We've got five school-free days to do anything we want," said Ross.

"Well I'm going to try along at the caves," said Simon. "Coming?"

"No. We never catch anything there."

Simon headed off across the rocky shoreline. He'd only been gone a few minutes when Ross heard him scream. Thinking his friend had fallen on the slippery rocks Ross hurried to his aid. But when he reached him, Simon was standing stock still, like a rabbit out-staring a pair of car headlights. He was gawking open mouthed at the statue of a girl. Ross had never seen such a life-like statue. From the freckles on her cheeks to the little cut on her left knee it was perfect in every detail. But the girl wore a terrified expression as if she'd been chased by little green men from a flying saucer.

"Wow," said Ross, meaning, "Crikey! What an absolutely amazing statue. It's so perfect it looks like a real girl who's been zapped by a quick-freeze ray as she ran across the rocks."

"It . . . it . . . it's Ann," stammered Simon. "It's Ann!"

"Ann?" quizzed Ross, "Ann who?"

"Ann Dromeda," replied Simon. "The girl you've been too cowardly to ask out on a date."

"I don't know what you're talking about."

"And you've forgotten Chris," said Simon pointing to another statue a short distance away.

"Wow!" said Ross, meaning, "This is the weirdest thing I've ever seen."

"Our friends are being turned to stone one by one."

"Wow!" said Ross, meaning, "Wow!"

"Will you stop saying 'wow' and help me work out what's going on."

The two boys thought for some time, trying to make sense of their discovery. Simon felt a strange mix of happiness, fear and excitement. He was happy that he wasn't going crazy and friends really were disappearing. This also sent a shiver of fear zapping up and down his spine. But most of all he was excited—this was the most awesome thing that had happened in all his life and somehow he sensed that the adventure was just beginning.

Ross interrupted his thoughts, "Do you remember a few weeks ago Miss Teryee told us some Ancient Greek myths?"

"Don't be silly, I never listen to anything Miss Teryee says."

"Well she told us about a Greek woman called Medusa. She was so frighteningly ugly that anyone who looked into her face turned to stone."

"Wow! That's cool," said Simon. "What else?"

"I don't know," replied Ross. "I wasn't really listening. I was busy throwing pencils at Alice."

Now, I don't expect that any of your friends have ever been turned to stone. As far as I know none of mine have. But one thing I'm sure of, if I ever found a friend turned to stone I would run straight home and stay in bed for a week. But fortunately Simon and Ross are not like me. Perhaps it's because they are adventurous and brave. Perhaps it's because they don't know the meaning of fear (actually there are thousands of words they don't know the meaning of). But they didn't run home and spend a week in their beds—which is a good thing for had they done so this story would be rather short and have a very boring ending. No, they decided to go and search in the dark and eerie caves for the evil person or creature that was turning their friends to stone. Brave—maybe. Foolish—definitely.

CHAPTER 5
Simon and Ross meet the girl with the world's worst hair style

There were two caves. To save time, Simon insisted they split up and explore one each. Ross took a coin.

"Heads you explore the creepy cave that's haunted by the evil ghosts of pirates—Tails I explore the bright shallow one where we shelter when it rains."

"Okay," said Simon. "Just hurry."

Ross threw the coin—Tails.

Simon squeezed through the narrow entrance. Immediately the darkness wrapped a hostile veil around him. The cold, thin air stabbed his lungs. Reaching out to steady himself, his fingers met a thick gooey substance trickling down the cave wall.

'Dead pirate's blood!' Simon screamed, but he was so terrified the words stuck in his throat and refused to come out. 'Don't be stupid—there's no ghosts . . . no blood,' he assured himself.

Still, he avoided touching the wall as he crept deeper into the cave. The passageway twisted this way and that and was strewn with rocks that reached out to trip him up. After a long upward climb the path gradually leveled out. Ahead, the cave opened out, lit by a shaft of light shimmering from above. Simon instinctively sensed danger. Not ghostly danger but definitely danger of some sort. His heart raced. Beads of fear tricked down his cheeks. Desperately he fought to control his breathing in case the sound of his gasping should betray him. He edged towards the light with foreboding.

"Aaarghhh!" screamed Simon.

"Aaarghhh!" screamed the girl at precisely the same time.

For a few moments of shock induced silence they stared at each other.

"You scared me!" exclaimed the girl.

"I scared you?" snapped Simon. "You're the one with snakes growing out of your head!"

"Oh that's right, start getting personal," said the girl indignantly.

"Well you must admit it's a bit unusual."

"Okay, so I'm having a bad hair day," said the girl. "Big deal."

Just at that moment Ross appeared out of the darkness.

"Aaarghhh" he screamed.

"Don't you start," said the girl.

"Yeah . . . have you never seen someone with snakes in their hair?" taunted Simon.

"B ... bu ... but it's Medusa," gasped Ross. "We'll turn to stone."

"Don't be ridiculous," said the girl, "if you were going to turn to stone you'd have done so immediately."

"Why haven't we?" asked Simon.

"How should I know?" said the girl. "Probably those silly sunglasses are protecting you."

"Why did you turn our friends to stone?" demanded Simon.

"That's right blame me," retorted the girl.

"So it wasn't you?" asked Ross.

"Well actually it was," said the girl, "but I didn't mean to."

"How can you turn people to stone without meaning to?" asked Simon.

"I'm not normally like this. I don't usually turn people to stone—if you must know," said the girl huffily.

"Turning one of my friends to stone is bad enough," said Simon, "but turning four to stone is unforgivable."

"I suppose I'd better explain," said the girl. "But first you must promise to help me."

"Why should we help you?" asked Simon.

"Because unless you do, your family, and friends will all be turned into monsters like me."

"That seems a pretty good reason," said Ross.

"Yeah . . . we'll help you . . . maybe," said Simon.

"Maybe is not good enough," said the girl. "You must promise."

"Okay," replied Simon. "We promise to definitely, maybe help you."

CHAPTER 6
Melissa tells an unbelievable story
that Simon and Ross believe

T he children made their way out of the cold, dank caves and headed for the beach. As they climbed across the rocks they introduced themselves. Simon didn't lie—for he was not that type of boy. But he may have exaggerated just a little for, when he'd finished talking, Melissa had the impression that he was a highly successful entrepreneur with a thriving internet business and that he lived alone in a castle. This of course was nonsense for we know that he was a not-very-successful schoolboy who lived with rather eccentric parents and had a crush on a girl who had recently been turned to stone. Ross said simply that he was twelve, collected worms and had won this year's Scottish Junior Chess Championship. All of which was true—and didn't cause anyone to think he was an astronaut.

The girl said her name was Melissa and she was eleven years old. She told the boys that she lived with her parents and little sister, Amanda, in the little village of Lochlinda on the island of Gogha where there were just forty-two adults and twelve children.

"So what about the snakes?" said Simon rather insensitively? "Why do you have snakes in your hair?"

"I guess I'd better tell you the awful thing that happened and why I need your help," said Melissa, as they made themselves comfortable on the sand.

Simon couldn't take his eyes off her. Although she had snakes in her hair, she was a pretty girl with silky skin and sparkling eyes— not the petrifying ugly Medusa that Ross had described. He stared at the snakes thrashing about on her head. They were fascinating— almost hypnotic to watch. He decided that although having snakes in your hair was completely weird, surprisingly it wasn't completely repulsive. He tried to count them but they moved so quickly it was impossible—he guessed there were about twelve.

"Yes," he said, checking his Ultra-Accurate-Atomic-Wrist-Watch. "This would be a good time for you to tell us the whole story."

"I'll start at the very beginning," said Melissa, "for I've always found that a particularly good place to start. About a year ago a strange stranger came to the island. He was a decrepit old man with a face as wrinkled as a rhinoceros. My best friend, Jillian, said he must be at least five-hundred years old but I guess he was only about eighty. He had sad sunken eyes, which made you feel that he was searching your soul and reaching right into your mind. He dressed completely in black and carried a crooked black cane. We nicknamed him Gloom. He turned up outside our school one day and asked some really odd questions."

"Like what?" interrupted Ross.

"Well he asked Jillian if she'd ever considered becoming a crocodile. Then he asked Andrew, a boy I don't particularly like, if he thought it was possible to make a dog fly. That horrid beast, Andrew, replied 'if you throw it hard enough'. This angered Gloom and he hobbled away on his stick muttering 'You nasty little whippersnappers—like all the others you laugh at me. But soon you will be my pets—then it will be my turn to laugh'. It was ever so creepy and we all decided to keep well clear of the old man. But next day he was gone.

We'd almost forgotten him when, about a month later, a rumor went around the village that he'd bought Mount Taine and Castle Taine from Lord McGready. Soon afterwards workmen arrived on the island and built an electrified fence right around the base of the mountain—it took them eight weeks. They put up signs that said 'Keep out or be FRIED'. Then Gloom returned. He appeared at the village shop, bought just about everything in it, and went to his castle on the slopes of the mountain. After that he was only ever seen when he went to the village shop for supplies or to pick up packages from the post office. About six weeks ago, cats and dogs started going missing. Gloom, of course, was blamed even though there was no proof that he was the culprit. My cat, Snowy was one of the first to disappear."

"What kind of cat is it?" asked Ross.

"A Ragdoll," replied Melissa.

"What color?" asked Ross.

"Pure white," said Melissa. "That's why I called her Snowy."

"I've got a cat," said Ross. "He's a brilliant rat catcher. That's why I call him . . ."

"For goodness sake," interrupted Simon, glaring at Ross. "You're wasting time. Can we get back to the story?"
Melissa scowled at Simon. Her snakes wriggled angrily. Hissing loudly they sprang out. Several forked tongues struck Simon's face before the snakes recoiled. He shifted uneasily in the sand.

"Please . . . please . . . continue in your own time," he said, backing away a little.

"A few days ago my friend, Jillian, came running to my house," Melissa continued. "She was shaking with fear. She'd been searching for her dog and spotted something on the other side of the electric fence. Although she only glimpsed it for a few seconds she was sure it was a creature with the body of a cat and the head of an oversized chicken. This proved our suspicions were right—Gloom was kidnapping our pets to experiment on. We told our parents but they said we were being silly. So we decided to tackle Gloom ourselves."

"That was brave," said Simon.

"What did you do?" asked Ross excitedly.

"First we put on rubber boots so that we wouldn't get electrocuted on the fence. It was difficult to climb and I ripped my skirt on the barbed wire. But we got over. We thought it would be safer to take the route through the woods. That way we were less likely to be seen. It was gloomy and creepy. The trees seemed to close in on us and every snapping twig made us jump. We imagined that every shadow and every sound was a monster coming to kill us. Several times we almost turned back but, although we were terrified, we made it to the castle. To our surprise the door was open. We crept along the dim corridors, peeping into each room, not really knowing what we were looking for. The place was empty. Not a trace of man or beast. Then we saw a sign, 'Doctor X's Top Secret Laboratory. Do not enter or ELSE!' Cautiously we pushed the door open a little and peered in. There was no one there. We crept inside."

"What did you find?" asked Ross.

"The first thing we saw was a table running the whole length of the room. On it stood rows of beakers being heated by little gas burners—just like in the school science lab. I felt disgusted when I saw what was in them. Bubbling up in the colorful liquids were eyes and brains and other disgusting bits of animals. The vile smell of decaying flesh made us wretch so we hurried away. At the far end of the room there was a large desk. Piled on top were dusty old magic books, books on mythology and lots of modern science books. In the centre of the desk was a large leather bound book. Written in gold were the words "The practice of scigic for evil and monstrous pleasure by Doctor A X."

"What's scigic?" asked Ross.

"It took us a while to puzzle that out," replied Melissa, brushing a snake out of her eyes. "It's the first three letters of science and the last three letters of magic. We worked out that Gloom was using a mixture of ancient magic and modern science and the book was the record of his ghastly experiments. I lifted it from the desk but was shaking so much I dropped it. It fell to the floor with a thud causing an echo that boomed around the room. We hid for a few moments in case anyone heard. But no one came in. We sat cross legged on the floor and excitedly turned the first page. There was a sketch of a nasty looking creature with the body of a wolf and the head of a gorilla. Underneath was a complex formula to change a person's DNA to produce this horrid beast.

"Wow!" said Ross. "What was the formula?"

"It was much too difficult for us to understand but the ingredients we recognized included; left eye of newt, one gram of calcium, heart torn from a live frog at midnight, two grams of potassium, beak of vampire bat, and a pinch of salt. And there was a magic spell to be recited while mixing the ingredients, it went something like:

Azparagiis, Vampiremus and other magic stuff,
Sometimes science is just not enough,
Charge this potion with the powers of old,
To turn all it quenches into creatures untold."

Simon looked at his Ultra-Accurate-Atomic-Wrist-Watch. "Time's slipping away," he said. "Can you give us the quick version?"

"Okay! Okay!" said Melissa. "Don't be so grumpy."

"He's always like this," said Ross.

"Well if you're going to be grumpy I'm not telling you any more," said Melissa.

"And if you take all day to tell us we're not going to be able to help you," snapped Simon.

"Keep your hair on," said Melissa.

"And you keep your snakes on," hissed Simon.

"Alright, alright, I'll try to be brief," sighed Melissa.

Slowly she adjusted her skirt and fiddled with her boots as if to show Simon she wouldn't be hurried. At last she continued.

"As we studied the book we heard a noise from a crate beneath the desk. A meowing sound. Jillian said it must be the kidnapped cats. For one wonderful moment I thought I'd get Snowy back. We opened the lid a fraction. It wasn't cats. It was vile bat-like creatures with large bony wings and huge mouths full of razor sharp teeth. Before we could slam the lid shut dozens had escaped. They attacked us—snapping at our hands and faces. One sunk its long fangs deep into my neck and began sucking my blood. Screaming I grabbed hold of it and pulled as hard as I could. It refused to let go. The pain was agonizing. I became dizzy. I was about to faint. In desperation I squeezed the horrid thing. It screeched in pain as I tried to crush it. Then, with a piercing hiss, it released its grip. The hideous creature squirmed about in my hand thrusting its toothy mouth at me in an effort to bite my fingers. It was slimy and its sharp bones dug into my skin. I threw it with all my strength against a wall. It flopped to the ground as if it was dead. But then I heard the sickening snapping of bones as its ribs shattered and its stomach burst open. Out of the blood and guts spewed about twenty new creatures. They all joined in the attack.

Terrified we fled from the room with the creatures chasing after us. As we ran along the corridor Doctor X appeared. We barged past him knocking him flying. We kept running until we reached the door. It was locked. Then something hit the back of my neck—a little dart. It must have been a tranquilizer for the next thing I remember is being back in the lab. I was tied up. Jillian was beside me. She was tied up too.

Smiling an evil grin Doctor X said, "Welcome to my laboratory, I'm glad you've decided to help me with my experiments."

CHAPTER 7
Simon and Ross get involved in a daring and dangerous adventure

A s Melissa told her story, Ross interrupted more and more frequently and Simon became more and more irritated at him for wasting time. Melissa was right about Gloom—he was an evil scientist. His real name was Doctor X—pronounced 'Z'. (He had been born in the French village of Y to unimaginative parents, Mr. and Mrs. X. They gave their new son the name A—the very same name as his brother and two sisters. It was because of his silly, short name that, as a child, A developed hippopotomonstrosesquippedaliophobia—the fear of long words.)

When A grew up he called himself Doctor X, even though he'd flunked all his school exams. He became obsessed with finding a way to create mutations of animals and humans. After decades of failed research, he finally discovered that a combination of ancient magic and modern science could be used to genetically modify animals. (This happened by chance when he accidentally dropped chemicals on a mouse and exclaimed angrily, 'Darn and blast my potassium has splashed' which, by remarkable coincidence was, in old Voodoo language, a particularly unpleasant curse. The mouse immediately grew an extra head—where its tail had been.) It was Doctor X's dream to use his new science, scigic, as he called it, to create mythical creatures.

The scientific world had shunned Doctor X, in fact most respectable scientists thought he was mad. In a cruel mocking way

29

they called Doctor X, Doctor X (pronounced 'X'). Often after long science conferences they would spend the evening drinking whisky and just saying his name over and over. They found this hysterical and would laugh for hours. I should point out that scientists have a very poor sense of humor—you would never hear one tell a knock-knock joke. The eminent science magazine 'Science for Amazingly Clever People' summed up their feelings in an article entitled, "Doctor X is mad—Scigic is silly." Doctor X was furious and vowed to get revenge. He bought Castle Taine so that he could carry out his experiments in secret. And once he had perfected scigic he planned to take over the world.

Melissa and Jillian couldn't have chosen a worse moment to be caught by Doctor X. His animal experiments had been successful and he was ready for the next step in his evil plan. Melissa and Jillian were to become his first human victims.

Melissa went on with her story, "Chanting a magic spell, Doctor X mixed some scigic serum. He forced me to drink a vile pink liquid and Jillian to drink a blue liquid. Immediately I began to quiver. Pulses, like electricity, surged through me. It was as if every single cell in my body was being energized. A strange sensation began in my stomach, as if birds were inside me flapping their wings. The feeling got stronger. It rose into my chest and, after a few painful flutters, it gushed through my throat and squeezed into my head. For an instant I thought my skull was exploding. Then everything felt normal.

That's when I heard Jillian shriek, 'Yuch! You've got snakes growing out of your head.'

'Oh you can talk,' I replied, feeling most indignant, 'you've grown wings and an ugly crooked beak.' She looked ever so funny—if I hadn't been so terrified I'd have laughed.

Doctor X shouted 'Yippeee!' and jumped up and down. He

studied us, as if we were a couple of laboratory rats, then he yelled,

'My years of insane, evil experimentation have all been worthwhile. I have created Medusa and Aello. I am a genius. Today Gogha will be mine. Tomorrow the world will be mine.'"

"Aello?" said Simon, "Who's Aello."

"Didn't you listen to anything Miss Teryee told us," scolded Ross. "Aello was a wicked mythological creature employed by the Ancient Gods to cruelly punish naughty boys and girls."

"Sorry for asking," said Simon, flashing Melissa a smile.

"Doctor X took several bottles from his desk," continued Melissa. "Adjusting his mirrored sunglasses he sneered at us saying, 'Now I will put my scigic serum into the island's water supply. Soon all your horrid little friends will become my mythical creatures. He he ha ha ha.'

As soon as he'd gone, I said to Jillian that we must escape and warn the villagers. Jillian managed to cut through her own ropes with her ugly crooked beak. She started pecking at mine but I could tell that the serum was still working on her. Her personality was changing—she was becoming evil. She stopped pecking my ropes. She shrieked at me in some weird language and started attacking my snakes. I begged her to stop but she wouldn't listen. Fortunately the ropes around my wrists were almost completely cut through and I managed to break them. With Jillian still pecking my snakes, I eventually managed to unbind my legs.

I backed away from her. But I didn't know what to do. My friend was now an evil monster. I didn't want to desert her but I didn't want to be killed by her either. She flapped her wings and thrust her head at me. Her ugly crooked beak struck me on the ribs. It was really painful. Jillian was raging with angry—she obviously wanted to kill me. I had no other choice. I ran for my life."

Ross had been warned not to interrupt but he couldn't restrain himself anymore—he had to butt in, "If your friend became evil, why didn't you?"

"I've had a lot of time to think about that," said Melissa, "but I still can't work out why."

"Although you've got snakes in your hair you're really beautiful. Not at all like Medusa from mythology," said Ross. He blushed at calling Melissa beautiful. He looked down so she couldn't see his face. "So maybe the scigic didn't work properly."

"That would be good," said Melissa, not noticing Ross's blushes. "For if it sometimes doesn't work, there could be creatures on the island willing to help us rather than kill us."

Simon stared at his watch. He didn't have to say a word. Melissa immediately got back to her story.

"Jillian chased after me. But she couldn't control her wings. She hit the ceiling. She smashed against walls. She bounced off furniture. As fast as I could, I sprinted along the corridors, out of the castle and slammed the door behind me. I kept running until I got to the village. But I was too late. It was already full of terrifying creatures. I didn't see a single normal person. I thought of trying to get home to phone for help but it was too dangerous and, to be honest, I couldn't even think of a single person I could phone. So I found a little boat and fled to the mainland. It was getting dark and I was exhausted by everything that had happened. I knew about the caves so I took shelter in one. I stayed there overnight, unable to sleep for worry and fear and because having snakes constantly slithering about on your head is something that takes a lot of getting used to."

"I wouldn't mind having snakes in my hair," said Simon, "That would sure stop that brute Brutus from bullying me."

"Don't interrupt," said Ross sarcastically.

Simon kicked Ross.

"In the morning I went looking for help," said Melissa. "I saw a boy walking along the beach. I called to him but as soon as he looked at me he turned to stone. It was awful. I felt terrible."

"Not as terrible as poor Chris must have felt," sniggered Simon.

"Over the next couple of days I tried several times to get help. But each time I met someone they turned to stone. I really began to despair."

"Then we turned up," said Simon, "Like two knights in shining armor come to rescue you."

"More like two halfwits in silly sunglasses, come to annoy me," said Melissa.

For a while the three sat in silence, deep in thought. Ross was first to speak.

"We should phone our parents or the police for help."

"Brilliant idea," said Simon. "But for one we don't have phones and for two, three, four and five that idiot of a Chief would really mess things up. He'd end up blowing up the island and everyone on it. And do you really think our parents would know what to do?"

"But this is too dangerous for us to tackle on our own," said Ross.

"Coward," said Simon.

"I'm not," said Ross.

"Are so," said Simon.

"I'm not," said Ross, "I just think the police . . ."

"This needs cunning and intelligence," interrupted Simon, "The Chief of Police couldn't even pick his own nose without a training manual."

"Simon's right," said Melissa. "Doctor X won't listen to anyone in authority but maybe . . . maybe if we plead with him . . ."

"I guess we've got no option but to help you," said Simon. "We must risk everything to go with you on this daring and dangerous adventure and are more likely to suffer a torturous and horrific death than return alive."

Ross frowned. He shook his head slowly from side to side but remained silent.

"When shall we start?" asked Melissa solemnly.

Simon looked at his Ultra-Accurate-Atomic-Wrist-Watch. "Now," he said.

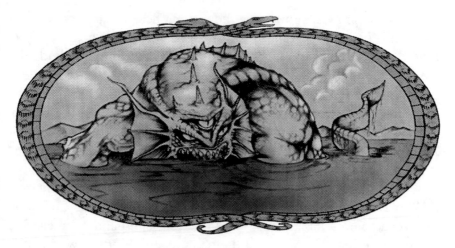

CHAPTER 8
In which the Children get into a spin over a sea monster

S imon, Ross and Melissa climbed into the little rowing boat. Simon pushed his way to the middle and took charge of the oars.

"Melissa, you sit at the back," he said, a little over insistently.

"You're not afraid of my snakes are you?" asked Melissa.

"Oh no, I love deadly animals," replied Simon, "but I much prefer them locked up in cages."

As the boat pulled away from the shore the boys looked back, wondering if they would ever see their parents again. Melissa looked at Gogha and wondered if her family were now diabolical monsters who would soon be trying to kill her. They journeyed in silence.

There was no wind and the sea was like glass. Simon was confident with boats and before long they were nearing the island. As they got close occasional noises shattered the silence; eerie roars and savage growls similar to those you hear at a zoo—only a thousand times louder and a zillion times scarier. Then, softly at first, they heard the strangest noise of all—sweet singing. Gradually the sound engulfed them. Although it remained soft and gentle it somehow blotted out all other sounds—blotted out their thoughts. They lost all fear of the creatures that awaited them on the island. They lost all desire to go to Ghoga and save the world from Doctor X. Now they had only one desire—to reach the source of the singing. Simon turned the boat away from the shore and rowed up the coastline. A short distance ahead a beautiful sea nymph sat on a rock playing a golden harp. Her skin was azure blue and long sea-weed colored hair flowed down her back in gentle waves. She smiled sweetly as she watched them approach. Simon rowed faster. As her song was in Greek they couldn't understand the words but even if they had it would have made no difference. They were spellbound-trapped by the nymph's wondrous voice as she sang her enchanting song . . .

Come children,
Come one by one,
Come to my seaweed wonderland.
My sea-horses will serve you,
A feast of oyster and caviar,
As you rest your weary heads,
On pillows made from turtle-shell.
And the cod will dance,
And the salmon will sing,
And you my dears will have everything.
Come children,
Come to my seaweed wonderland,
Come, come, come to your graves.

From the still water an enormous head rose up. A green scaly head with a mouth so big it could swallow fifty men in one go without the use of a knife and fork. The children were so entranced by the song that they kept heading towards it. Three gigantic bulging eyes watched them approach. Just a few days earlier this fierce sea monster had been Melissa's mild mannered teacher, Miss Doogooder. Now she planned Melissa's demise. The monster lowered her head so that her mouth was below the surface. She breathed in sharply taking thousands of gallons of water into her huge belly. Then, with a thunderous explosion, she exhaled. The sea spun in a mighty whirlpool catching the little boat in its grip. Suddenly released from their trance by the ear-splitting roar of the waves they saw the terrifying three-eyed monster staring down at them. They screamed.

Faster and faster the boat raced in ever decreasing circles towards the sea monster. The beast watched like a cat toying with a mouse, waiting for the right moment to pounce. While Simon fought frantically to keep the little boat from capsizing, Melissa and Ross desperately gripped its sides to stop themselves being thrown overboard.

Once more the sea nymph's singing rose above the other sounds. Simon immediately fell under its spell and let go of the oars—the boat lurched over into the waves and water rushed in. Luckily Melissa realized what was happening. She knew she had to drown out the sound of the singing or become the monster's next meal.

"Keep rowing Simon," she yelled.

Simon remained motionless, oblivious to what was happening around him.

"Shout as loudly as you can," Melissa screamed at Ross.

Clutching on for their lives, as they were thrown from side to side, they inched towards the middle of the boat. They squeezed onto the seat beside Simon and bellowed into his ears.

"Come on Simon," roared Melissa. "This is no time to desert us."

"Simon, it's me, Ross," shrieked Ross. "Wake up—we're all going to be killed."

"Help us Simon. Help us . . ." pleaded Melissa.

The boat twisted and rolled out of control as it spun in dizzying circles. Three eyes watched. One massive tongue licked massive lips at the thought of the meal ahead.

"For goodness sake Simon," bellowed Melissa, "snap out of it."

"Why are you shouting in my ear?" Simon suddenly barked back.

"Don't ask," roared Melissa. "Just scream. Scream as loudly as you can until I tell you it's safe to stop."

The huge beast plunged under the water and sank to the sea bed. She turned, shot to the surface at great speed, head-butting the boat from below. The boat flew out of the water high into the air. The children's screams of terror turned to screams of absolutely horrific get-me-out-of-here terror. The boat twisted and turned in mid-air before plunging back into the water a short distance from shore.

"Row," shouted Melissa. "Row as fast as you can."

The monster rose out of the sea and eyed its prey. Now it was time to stop playing and move in for the kill.

"Faster!" screeched Melissa. "Faster!"

The monster charged at such speed a huge wake of water rose around her. The little boat was tossed from side to side like a leaf in a hurricane.

"Keep rowing," commanded Melissa.

The monster was almost upon them.

"Faster," screamed Melissa desperately. "Keep heading

towards the shore."

Simon did as he was told and, although the boat was being lashed by waves, managed to steer it towards the small bay.

"Come on," shrieked Melissa. "We're almost there."

The little boat smashed against a submerged rock and toppled over, jettisoning the children into the water. The sea monster gave an almighty roar of pain as her underbelly struck sharp rocks in the shallow water of the bay. Despite her injuries she desperately kept trying to swim—angry that her prey was getting away. But her attempts were in vain. The children scrambled, half swimming, half crawling, towards the shore. Just when they were about to reach safety the monster shot out a long tentacle. It wrapped around Ross's legs and held tight with powerful suckers. Ross struggled to free himself but he was no match for the beast—gradually he was dragged, screaming and shouting, away from the shore towards his death.

Simon threw himself back into the water and swam after his friend. He grasped Ross by the arms. A short distance from shore, where the sea was deeper, three bulging eyes peered from above the water and studied Simon pensively. A second tentacle slowly stretched out through the waves. Simon felt a slimy sucker wrap around his face—stealing his breath. Still gripping his friend, he kicked out and struck the tentacle. It recoiled a little. The tentacle stretched out once more, wrapped itself around Simon's chest and squeezed. Although he could barely breathe Simon kept kicking. The tentacle's grip tightened. Simon kicked out desperately. His heel struck hard against the under side of the tentacle. It split on impact. The sea monster yelped in pain. Slimy green blood oozed from the wound. The tentacle flopped, lifeless, on the surface of the water. Simon could breathe again. But the other tentacle continued to pull the boys towards a hungry mouth.

As they were dragged past the overturned boat, Simon grabbed an oar. In one slick motion he swam forward, raised the oar out of the water and smashed it down on the tentacle that was wrapped around Ross.

The monster groaned and for a moment stopped pulling. Simon whacked the oar down again and again and again. Gradually the tentacle loosened its grip. He kept on hitting the beast but every strike sapped his strength. The oar now felt like a lead weight pulling him to a watery grave. Simon summoned up his last fiber of energy. Arms aching, he raised the oar for one last strike. But, as he smashed it down, the monster groaned and gave up the fight. With a rasping curse it sank back to the depths to nurse its wounds. Ross and Simon swam, breathless, towards the shore.

"Keep shouting," Melissa reminded them as they pulled themselves out of the water. "Keep shouting till we get clear of the singing."

"I'm trying to," spluttered Ross. "But I'm half drowned."

Without looking back they clambered up the steep slope, squeezed between the bushes, and hurried away from the shore.

"Okay, you can stop shouting," panted Melissa. "We're safe now."

But Melissa was wrong!

CHAPTER 9
Mr. McRoast thinks the children are fast-food—but will they be fast enough?

Cold and afraid, the children shivered as they rested on the grass. The warm sun would soon dry out their clothes but it couldn't soothe their fears. Simon checked his Ultra-Accurate-Atomic-Wrist-Watch every few seconds but said nothing. Melissa's snakes thrashed about making her even more anxious. Ross's stomach churned with dread. He desperately wanted to run to the boat, find a safe way home and end this nightmare. But he knew he couldn't—he might not be very brave but he wasn't a quitter and he certainly wouldn't let his friends down. To make matters worse he was sure that something was watching them. He tried to convince himself that it was just his imagination but he twitched like Melissa's snakes as he scanned the bushes.

Ross' intuition was right. The village butcher, Mr. McRoast was examining them thoroughly in the way he once checked carcasses before chopping them into different cuts of meat. Mr. McRoast had always been a grumpy old man——the type of person you'd cross a highway to avoid. But since that cup of tea a few days earlier he'd become even grumpier, for the scigic in the water had changed him. Now he had the body of a lion and three heads, one a goat head, one a wolf head and the third an eagle head. And to make matters even worse——all three had headaches.

Mr. McRoast was pleased with his find. The children looked rather tender and would make three lovely meals. He resolved to follow them and, as soon as his heads decided when to eat, he would launch his attack.

CHAPTER 10
The children discover that genetically modified chickens are not all cute little bundles of fluff

"So what do we do now?" asked Ross.

"First we need to get to the castle," said Melissa.

"That won't be easy if we meet more creatures like that sea monster," said Simon.

"Don't worry," said Melissa. "The island is covered in woods. We can keep out of sight for most of the way."

"But what if there's a monster in the woods?" asked Ross.

"We'll let it eat you while we escape," said Simon, hunching over and making a face like a fierce monster.

"Oh thanks a lot," said Ross, sticking out his tongue.

"Well stop asking silly questions," said Simon.

"Wasn't a silly question," said Ross.

"Was," insisted Simon.

"Wasn't," said Ross.

"Will you two stop arguing," said Melissa.

"Yeah Ross, you're wasting valuable time," said Simon glancing at his Ultra-Accurate-Atomic-Wrist-Watch. "Look after the minutes . . . "

"And the stupid hours will look after themselves," interrupted Ross.

Simon elbowed Ross in the ribs. Ross kicked Simon on the bum. Simon punched his friend in the stomach.

"Stop it," snapped Melissa. "Come on, follow me——I know

the best route to the village. From there we can get to the castle."

Simon and Ross followed Melissa, still arguing and pushing each other as they wove their way around bushes and trees. With all the nimbleness of a grumpy old man who had just been given the body of a lion and three monstrous heads, Mr. McRoast followed. The three heads moaned quietly about how difficult it was to walk in a straight line when three different brains are telling one set of legs which direction to go. Every few minutes a head would bump against a tree—making its headache worse.

As they scurried along the pathway, Ross's sensation of being watched grew. Regularly he stopped and stared into the bushes.

"Will you stop stopping," bellowed Simon.

"Something's following us," said Ross. "I'm sure I can see eyes glistening in the bushes."

"If we are being followed the last thing we should do is stop," said Simon. "If we slow down it will stop following us and start eating us."

"I wish we'd brought knives or a couple of your dad's guns," said Ross.

"Yeah," agreed Simon, pretending he was blasting Ross with a sub-machine gun. "That way we could blast anything that got in our way."

"Hold on," said Melissa, "we can't harm any of these creatures."

"What!" exclaimed Ross.

"You never told us that before we offered to help," said Simon.

"Well I'm telling you now," said Melissa. "Any of the creatures could be one of my family or a friend."

A deafening roar split the air.

"Sounds like they're pleased to have you back," said Simon.

They walked the next few miles without saying a word—each feeling rather irritated with the others. The roaring and growling was becoming louder, clearly they were heading towards great danger.

"Stop," whispered Ross, just loud enough for Simon and Melissa to hear. "Something's moving in the bushes—I told you we're being followed."

They stopped and listened.

"It's chickens," said Simon sharply. "That's all—just chickens clucking."

Suddenly a group of about twenty funny looking creatures hopskipped out of the shrubs onto the path ahead of them. Simon was right, well partly right. The creatures had chicken heads but rabbit bodies. The children stood as still as toadstools in the hope that the creatures would keep running. But they didn't. They stayed on the path, pecking at the ground and occasionally doing silly little hops the way young rabbits do.

"They're ever so cute," said Melissa.

"I wonder if they lay eggs?" said Ross.

"Yeah. Easter Bunny eggs," said Melissa

"We're losing time," moaned Simon. "And we don't have any time to lose."

"Give them a few minutes and they'll probably hop off," said Melissa, settling down on the path to watch the little creatures. But after fifteen minutes and twelve seconds the creatures showed no sign of shifting and Simon was becoming broody.

"We need to do something," he said. "The shrubbery is too dense to go around them. We'll have to chase them away."

"Won't that be dangerous?" asked Ross.

"They're chickens for goodness sake," said Simon. "What harm can they do?"

So, reluctantly, Melissa and Ross agreed to chase them. Simon counted down, "three . . . two . . . one . . . go."

They charged towards the strange little creatures at top speed. Now, normally a chicken would lay an egg at the sight of three humans running at it but these were obviously no ordinary chickens. They turned to face the children. Their cute expressions changed to that of hostile aggression. They gurgled noisily as if clearing their throats then began spitting slimy mucus pellets. Hundreds struck the children's legs at high speed and stung like crazy. But they were running too fast to stop and soon were in the middle of the creatures.

"Keep running," commanded Simon.

And they did—with the creatures still spitting at them. By the time they were clear, their legs were cut, aching and dripping with red and green mucus. They found a stream and washed away the sickening slime. Using dock leaves, picked from the edge of the stream, Melissa rubbed their wounds. Gradually the pain eased. But the three had learned an important lesson. The creatures on the island were deadly dangerous—no matter how cute they looked.

CHAPTER 11
Me's wants me's dinner

"Me's hungry," moaned the Eagle Head.

"You can't be," snapped the Goat Head.

"Well me is," said the Eagle Head.

"You ate yesterday," said the Wolf Head.

"Me knows when me's hungry," said the Eagle Head. "And that was just a snack."

Mr. McRoast plodded stealthily between the bushes keeping just within scent of his prey.

"Left here," thought the Eagle Head.

"Straight ahead," thought the Wolf Head.

"Let's check out that nice little bush," thought the Goat Head. Mr. McRoast stumbled and, for the umpteenth time that day, caught his fur on sharp thorns.

"This is awful," he thought—with all three heads at once.

"Me's eat the little one," pleaded the Eagle Head.

"Not now," said the Goat Head.

"Yeah cool it," said the Wolf Head.

"Why do yours get to decide?" asked the Eagle Head.

"Because," said the Wolf and Goat Heads in unison.

"Because what," said the Eagle Head.

"Just because," said the Wolf and Goat Heads.

"Not fair," said the Eagle Head.

"Stop moaning," said the Wolf Head.

"When me's do eat one," said the Eagle Head, "can me's eat

the little one first?"

"All right," said the Goat Head. "Now shut-up."

CHAPTER 12
Ross discovers that it's never a good idea to cheer fighting monsters

The children continued their journey with increased caution, wary of every sound and movement in the trees and shrubs around them. After two unadventurous miles they came to the edge of the woods. They peered out from the relative safety of the last few bushes. The village was just a short distance away across an open field. There were no creatures in sight. They watched for a few minutes, checking carefully in every direction—but saw nothing. They made a run for it. Simon was by far the fastest of the three. He hated going slowly, but he kept pace with his friends for though he often fought with Ross, in a way he felt protective of him—and Melissa, well she was a year younger and had snakes in her hair so she definitely needed protection.

They got to Main Street safely. It too was empty. Warily they stole along Church Street then took the hilly road up School Lane towards the Common. Still nothing to be seen. Their confidence rose. Perhaps getting to the castle wouldn't be as difficult as they had feared. They ran past the school to where the lane opened out onto the Common. All three gasped as if air was suddenly in short supply. They froze on the spot. They stared with unblinking eyes. The Common was alive with mythical creatures; some resting, some eating, many fighting.

Simon broke the trance. "Let's get away from here," he whispered.

Like actors in a movie being played in slow motion, they crept to the safety of a garden wall. Trembling they peered over. There, in front of them, was the weirdest collection of creatures imaginable. There were ogres and unicorns, dragons and griffins; creatures with animal bodies and huge wings. Many were a mix of two, three or more different animals. Some had more than one head. It was as if they'd stumbled across some Martian Circus Freak Show. Most frightening of all were the creatures the size of giant dinosaurs.

"What are we going to do?" asked Ross.

"I don't know," grumbled Simon.

"We'll never make it across the Common in one piece," said Melissa.

Secretly she wiped her tears—not wanting the boys to think she was weak. These were the first tears she'd shed since this nightmare had started. Until now she'd been confident that everything would eventually work out alright. Even when she'd turned the children to stone she was sure that, when she pleaded with Doctor X, he'd fix everything.

Her head spun, as a cocktail of emotions swirled around— each demanding attention; "I want my mom and dad . . . I need to be brave . . . any of these monsters could be my sister . . . I need to fix this out but how? . . . I'm not brave . . . I can't do this . . . I'm probably going to be eaten by one of my friends . . . please let me wake up and find that this is just a horrid dream . . . but this isn't a dream . . . I have no choice . . . I need to stop Doctor X . . ."

She choked back her tears. A thin smile spread across her face. "So what do you think of my family and friends," she whispered.

Suddenly from close by came a thunderous roar. Two creatures were squaring up for a fight. Although there was no way Melissa could have known, one of these was her headmaster, Professor Punnygiver and the other a boy called Andrew. Remember he's the one that Melissa didn't like—the boy who had been cheeky to Doctor X. It would have delighted Melissa to know that he'd been turned into an ugly monster and that Professor Punnygiver had been changed into the giant Argus Panoptes.

Ross stood on tiptoe to get a better view. The two creatures stomped the ground, growling at each other in a show of aggression. Professor Punnygiver was now four meters high and despite his efforts to appear fierce he still looked like a gentle giant. He had a kind face with a pointed beard and long flowing white hair. Now you may think that your teacher has eyes in the back of his head but the Professor really did—in fact he had one-hundred eyes. He had eyes on his arms and legs. He even had a couple on his bum. The great thing about having so many eyes, apart from always knowing what color of underwear you're wearing, is that it's possible to sleep with ninety-eight of them closed and watch out for enemies approaching with the other two. This was very useful on monster filled Gogha.

Andrew looked like a two headed tyrannosaurus but with two long necks protruding from a massive lizard-like body. From heads to claws he was six meters high. On each head Andrew had one gigantic round eye. His huge jaws were so powerful he crushed rocks with them just for fun. Even in his new form Andrew was a bully who enjoyed picking on smaller creatures.

Ross carefully weighed up the opponents; he wanted the Professor to win but thought the chances of that happening were zilch.

The fight began with some playful head butting. Andrew struck the Professor first. A stomach-churning thud rang out across the common. Quickly a crowd of beasts gathered to watch.

"ξις έκ ξιςΦέκ," said Andrew. (Which is Ancient Greek for "Fight, you big sissy.")

The Professor fought back. Ducking and diving to avoid being hit he tried to smash his opponent's thick skulls. But his head-butting was weak and off target.

"οίον ίπο βρηβρη στέ," growled the Professor. ("Stand still you two headed freak.")

Having the advantage of two heads, Andrew could head-butt twice as often. After suffering a torrent of skull crunching blows, the Professor swayed dizzily from side to side. Desperately he tried to block the attack but he was no match for Andrew. He was on the verge of defeat, before the fight had really begun in earnest.

"ητ αζσης βᵀᵇρ οον ρέβκηλέ," teased Andrew. ("Are you fighting or dancing?")

"The beast with the eyes is getting pulverized," whispered Ross. "Why doesn't it punch its opponent?"

"Shusssshhh," hissed Simon, "or I'll punch you."

As if reading Ross's thoughts the Professor changed tactics. He let out the loudest roar he could muster in an effort to frighten his opponent. Andrew roared back—refusing to be intimidated. The onlooking beasts stepped back to avoid being trampled as the battle heated up.

"νέκ βρέθνλέ έθ ξκν ξιξς," said the Professor. ("Here's some dance moves you've never seen before.")

He rushed forward. Nimbly he dodged Andrew's advancing heads and ducked beneath his outstretched necks. With big bony fists, he landed blow upon blow onto Andrew's scaly chest. Winded, Andrew for a moment couldn't fight back.

"νέξν θν ζηα κ λέλέλέ ιέθέθέθ," sneered the Professor. ("I call this dance the Jitter-Bug Hit-a-Thug.")

The Professor kept punching. Andrew tried to punch back but his tiny arms couldn't reach their target. Andrew roared again—this time in pain. Dazed by the onslaught of punches he meekly dropped his heads. A bad mistake. This gave the Professor an even better target. He took aim and unleashed a torrent of rage upon his opponent. One fierce blow struck the eye on Andrew's left head—immediately it puffed up and turned orange. The Professor became a blur.

"Δ εξεα ηζα εε," laughed the Professor. ("You didn't see that one coming.")

"Nice one," whispered Ross.

Simon punched him on the arm.

Andrew raged—he'd never lost a fight before and wasn't about to do so now. With the strength only found in anger, he fought through his pain. He lashed out, grabbing the Professor's arms— one in each mouth. He swung him backwards and forwards, then released him into the air. The Professor rose high above the onlookers before crashing back to the ground. His head took the full force.

"Δόςό ηπςό ύλς Δε," jeered Andrew. ("It's me your fighting not the grass, Stupid.")

"Oh no," thought Ross but didn't dare utter a sound.

The Professor lay motionless—almost unconscious. Andrew gave a triumphant roar. But behind him his opponent was struggling to his feet. Silently the Professor crept forward and sprang onto Andrew's back. Grabbing a neck he squeezed with all his might.

"νέεξ κ εα β ξβν ξυς έβρηθ," said the Professor. ("The view from here sure takes your breath away.")

With his right air supply cut off, Andrew coughed and spluttered as he struggled to breathe. He wobbled from side to side almost collapsing into the crowd. With one last desperate effort, he threw himself to the ground—landing on top of the Professor. The weight of Andrew's massive body bore down on the Professor's chest, crushing his ribs but with a powerful twisting motion he rolled free. Grasping Andrew's heads he thumped them together again and again. The noise, like a war drum, rang out as a warning not to mess with the Professor. Andrew flopped in a heap—unconscious. The Professor stamped his feet and let out a victory roar. The battle was over.

"Well done," yelled Ross, so excited that for a moment he forgot where he was.

That's how the Minotaur spotted them.

CHAPTER 13
Running scared from Minotaur to Minotaur

Now you probably haven't seen a Minotaur before. Oh you may have seen them in drawings but it's unlikely that you'd be particularly scared by those. But have you stood face to face with one with its acrid breath burning into your skin? Has one charged at you with its sharp horns thrust forward, ready to gorge the intestines right out of your body? No. I thought not. Well the Minotaur is one of the fiercest beasts in mythology. It has the body of a man and the head of a bull. Now that may sound more funny than fierce. But what if I told you that it's twelve feet tall, with the muscles of an Olympic weight-lifter and that its bull-head is double the size of a normal bull head with teeth that could tear off your leg in one playful bite? Beginning to get the idea?

Snorting, the Minotaur looked the intruders up and down. He bent forward so that his massive horns were ready for the onslaught. The smooth sharp tips glistened ominously in the sunshine. Roaring in a voice half-human, half-bull, he charged. The children fled in the direction they'd come from. The beast raced after them snorting with rage—steam fuming from his nostrils. Aroused by the excitement of a chase other creatures joined in.

"Come on Ross, you need to run faster," yelled Simon, as they stumbled awkwardly down the steep hill.
Ross glanced back.
"There are dozens of beasts chasing us," he yelled.
The roar of raging beasts shattered the air, hijacking the children's senses.
"Don't look. Keep running," commanded Simon.
The menacing sound of hooves closed in as the leading beasts gained ground.
"If I'm going to get killed by a weird creature I want to know what it looks like," panted Ross.
Driven on by the stench of fear the beasts jostled to be first to the kill.
"Stop arguing. Think of a way to escape," yelled Melissa.
They kept running; running for their lives. Ahead of them a second Minotaur leapt out from behind a parked truck. They crashed to a halt. They were trapped. In a matter of seconds their flesh would be ripped from their bones in a frenzied bloodbath.
"Stare at it," commanded Simon. "Stare at it and turn it to stone."
"I am staring," cried Melissa. "Nothing's happening."
"Well stare harder," bellowed Simon. "Come on Melissa."
Melissa stared straight into the huge beast's angry eyes willing it to turn to stone. With an eternity of hate the beast glared back. The rancid heat from his breath engulfed Melissa, burning her lungs with fear. The Minotaur's roar spat across her face. He obviously was not stone.
"It's not working," said Melissa.

"Oh great," said Simon, "You turn my friends to stone but your power won't work when we need it."

"Don't blame me," snapped Melissa.

"I've just remembered something Miss Teryee told us," said Ross. "Medusa's power only worked on humans. Animals and mythical beasts could stare at her all day without any nasty effect."

"Brilliant," groaned Simon.

Dozens of creatures were now crowded around, eager for a fight and the spilling of blood. The two Minotaurs pushed forward and scowled a warning to the others, claiming the quarry for themselves. Horns thrust out like swords they inched towards their victims.

"Come on," yelled Ross. "Through here."

Ross squeezed through a tiny gap in a garden hedge with Simon and Melissa fast on his heels.

"Faster, faster. Come on," shrieked Ross.

Behind them they heard the commotion as the Minotaurs tore the hedges from their roots.

The children scrambled over garden fences, clambered through rose-bushes and hedges and eventually, scratched and bruised, distanced themselves from their pursuers.

"This way," said Melissa, taking over the lead from Ross.

Eventually they reached Melissa's house and with the help of a brick, broke a window and climbed inside. It wasn't until they'd raided the refrigerator that they realized just how hungry they were. Melissa had barely eaten for days. They settled down to eat. Outside it was getting dark. They could go no further that day. While they ate they made plans. It was obvious that the route across the Common was impossible. According to Melissa there was only one alternative—to travel right around to the other side of the island, climb Mount Taine and approach the castle from the rear. None of the three liked the thought of that. They had no idea what creatures they might encounter—but there seemed no other choice. The decision was made. They would rest overnight and set out at dawn.

CHAPTER 14
Me's lost me's dinner

"Where's me's dinner gone?" asked the Eagle Head.

"Dunno," replied the Goat Head.

"Me's wants me's dinner," cried the Eagle Head.

"Stop complaining," said the Wolf Head.

"Well get me me's dinner," said the Eagle Head.

"Be patient," said the Goat Head. "We'll find the little lunch-packs again."

"Can me's eat them?" asked the Eagle Head.

"Soon," replied the Goat Head. "Soon."

CHAPTER 15
Borrowing bubble gum and jelly beans for the long journey

It was just after sunrise when Simon smashed down the door of the village shop. Feeling a little guilty he clambered inside, closely followed by Ross and Melissa.

"I've never stolen anything before," said Ross, as they crammed their backpacks full of essentials—cola, potato chips, jelly beans, bubble gum and chocolate.

"We're not stealing," insisted Melissa. "We're just borrowing."

"Well I don't think there's much chance of them getting these Green-Apple-Jelly-Beans back," said Simon stuffing a handful into his mouth.

"Anyway it was probably Mrs. Roode, the shop owner, who chased us down School Lane yesterday," said Melissa. "That fierce beast looked a lot like her and its bellowing voice certainly sounded like hers."

Almost all the mythical creatures were resting after a tiring evening fighting on the Common. The past few days had been a puzzling time for them. Having suddenly materialized out of nowhere, well out of the inhabitants and animals of the island to be more precise, they were still figuring out the pecking order. Some of the smaller creatures didn't get too involved in the fighting—except against other small beasts and mainly those much, much smaller than themselves. But the biggest creatures were keen to prove that they ruled the Common and so most evenings were devoted to fighting. Minotaur against Minotaur. Dragon against Dragon. Minotaur against Dragon and so on. As yet there was no clear victor—just a lot of creatures with lots of cuts and bruises—not to mention monstrously sore heads.

So the children reached the woods again completely unnoticed—except by one creature who, having three highly sensitive noses (and a keen interest in having child-burger for lunch), had detected their scent as they left the village shop.

They retraced their steps and it was still early morning when they reached the place where they'd escaped from the sea monster. Without a word being exchanged they each made a lot of noise as they hurried past the spot where the sea nymph had been. Rather than scream, this time they sang. They sounded like a choir of out-of-tune foghorns—though to be honest most foghorns would find this comparison very insulting.

Gradually the woods gave way to a dense stretch of forest. This offered them greater protection. As the trees were close together it would be difficult for the larger creatures to make their way through. But in the dark, with no path to follow, there was even greater danger of getting lost and their progress was difficult and slow.

"I need to rest," said Melissa after they'd walked five miles.

"Just a little further then we'll stop," said Simon.

"I can't go any further," said Melissa.

"Just one more mile," said Simon.

"No!" said Melissa.

Simon looked at Melissa. She was sweating in the heat and even her snakes looked exhausted.

"Okay," he agreed without further argument. "We'll stop for exactly one hour."

They found a clearing where the sunlight wasn't blocked by trees. There, a soft grassy patch provided the perfect place to sit. They each took a can of cola and some food from their rucksack. Simon had jelly beans, Ross some fruit chews and Melissa a much more sensible, peanut butter bar. But walking had made them hungry so they soon raided their bags for seconds.

"When will we reach the other side of the island?" asked Ross. Melissa thought for a considerable time and after some very complicated mental arithmetic involving Pythagora's theory, the size of the island and their estimated walking speed she replied, "Don't know."

"We'll need to be careful not to run out of food," said Simon.

"We should have brought more," said Ross.

"Oh right," snapped Simon. "And how would we have carried it?"

Ross made a face at Simon but didn't reply. The three sat in silence for a long time.

Suddenly Melissa's snakes became agitated as if they sensed danger. They reached out towards the trees and hissed irritably.

"Stop it," she commanded wearily. "We're safe here. Keep still."

The snakes stopped thrashing about and the children lay drowsily on the grass.

CHAPTER 16
Me's wants to attack me's dinner

Forward," thought the Eagle Head.

The huge Lion Body charged.

"Stop," thought the Wolf Head.

The huge Lion Body came to an abrupt halt just feet away from the sleeping children.

"Forward," thought the Eagle Head.

The Lion Body lurched forward.

"Stop," thought the Wolf Head.

"Forward," thought the Eagle Head.

"Stop," thought the Wolf Head.

"Forward," thought the Eagle Head.

"Stop," thought the Wolf Head. "Stop. Stop. Stop."

The Lion Body came to a complete halt and refused to listen to any further instructions.

"Me's attack the food," said the Eagle Head.

"No. Not yet," said the Goat Head.

"Yes!" demanded the Eagle Head.

"They're still ripening," said the Goat Head. "Give them a little more time."

"But me's hungry," said the Eagle Head.

"The feeling you have isn't hunger," explained the Wolf Head. "It's greed."

"When me's eat them?" asked the Eagle Head.

"Tomorrow," replied the Goat Head. "Maybe tomorrow."

CHAPTER 17
Danger, danger everywhere,
on the ground and in the air

After precisely one hour, Simon woke the others and they continued their journey, even though they'd rather have rested longer. Well, if the truth be known they'd rather have been home in bed, eating doughnuts, while watching television and chatting on the phone to a friend. Simon thought about his mom. He'd been away from home for over twenty-four hours. Would she be worrying about him? Would she be searching for him? Would she be crying and wailing at the loss of her only child? Would she be sorry now that she confiscated his cell phone? Simon decided that she wouldn't even have noticed that he was missing. Actually this was rather unfair on Mrs. Fairleywelthy, for in fact she had noticed he was missing. Only an hour earlier she'd said, "I'm starving—where's that good for nothing What's-His-Name gone?"

Ross's mom had worn out the bedroom carpet pacing up and down in her spiked climbing boots. She'd phoned the police, the army, the navy, the boy scouts, the air force, the British Prime Minister and the President of the United States and demanded they mount an international search.

"Get lost," each of them had said before hanging up.

Actually they hadn't all said, "Get lost". When she told the Chief of Police that the boys were missing he'd shouted, "Yippeeeeeeee" and rocked gleefully on his wooden rocking horse.

The children had made the decision to keep close to the sea and walk around the perimeter of the island. This wasn't the shortest route but it certainly reduced their chances of getting lost.

The further they got from the village the more convinced they became that they had chosen the right route. There were no eerie roars or savage growls so they became less and less cautious. Now instead of always keeping themselves hidden by trees and bushes, they'd sometimes take shortcuts across open fields. And, although Ross would occasionally get that we're-being-followed feeling and Melissa's snakes would sometimes become irritated, they had no idea that they were being followed by Mr. McRoast.

Now you are probably wondering why he hadn't eaten the children yet. I certainly thought it odd so I did a bit of checking on the internet. Mr. McRoast was now a Chimera—you'll remember that he has the body of a lion and three heads. Well I discovered that lions only eat once a week. On the day before the children had arrived Mr. McRoast had caught and eaten a small deer, so his stomach was full. The three heads—they're a different story. Wolves are used to going long periods without food so the Wolf Head was quite content to wait a few days before eating again. Eagles however like to eat several fish or rabbits every day—so that's why the Eagle Head was desperate to make a meal of the children. Goats prefer eating grass and shrubs so the children were of no interest to the Goat Head—and anyway whenever the other two heads weren't looking he would have a quick grassy snack.

Although Mr. McRoast was following the children with every intention of eating them very soon, he was not at this point their main threat. No, Elizabeth Marigold had been sitting on top of a tall fir tree watching them for some time. She was now the main danger. A few days earlier it had been Elizabeth's tenth birthday and she'd had a party with her best friends Alice and Hannah. The girls had spent the afternoon listening to music and arguing over who was the prettiest. Elizabeth poured drinks of cola chilled with ice— but after the first sip they began to transform. Before they got the chance to cut the cake all three girls had turned into Harpies— terrible monsters with the bodies of giant birds and the heads of ugly women. Elizabeth now had long straggly grey hair and a face that was so haggard even the wrinkles had wrinkles. Her smile revealed teeth so decayed maggots crawled amongst them. Alice had cropped blue hair and ears so big she could flap them to keep herself cool. She had so many warts on her face that they fought each other for breathing space. Hannah's most striking feature was a long twisted nose that constantly dripped yellowish-purple mucus. From time to time she licked it off with her long forked tongue. The girls now argued constantly about who was the ugliest. That's why Elizabeth was sitting all by herself on the tree—she'd squabbled with Alice and Hannah that afternoon for calling her cruel names like 'pretty', 'beautiful' and 'not completely hideous'.

Elizabeth Marigold flew from the top of the old oak tree to tell her friends about her find.

CHAPTER 18
A surprise attack by three ugly harpies who insist on making funny faces

"Wake up you lazy cretins," squawked Elizabeth.
"There are strange beasts in our woods."

Alice raised her head a little and opened one bloodshot eye.

"Get lost you big mommy's girl," she shrieked.

"Yeah go and make a nest with the pretty things," said Hannah.

Alice and Hannah were lying in the nest the three girls had built out of branches. It wasn't a particularly comfortable nest but it was home. And Alice and Hannah had no intention of leaving it—not for anything.

"Come on. Come on," shrieked Elizabeth. "You two never do nothing no more."

"It's fun just watching the clouds go by," said Alice.

"Or watching the trees grow," added Hannah.

"And what about the strange beasts?" asked Elizabeth. "Are you two going to lie back and let any old young thing trespass on our property?"

"Are they ugly beasts?" asked Hannah.

"No. They're very pretty little things," said Elizabeth.

"Oh well," Hannah yawned. "I guess we'd better go kill them."

Alice and Hannah hopped out of the nest onto nearby branches and stretched their repulsive wings.

"Let's make this quick," said Alice. "There's a nice black cloud coming along and I want to watch it float by."

Even as they flew to kill the children, the hideous Harpies couldn't help criticizing each other.

"You're looking exceptionally nice today Elizabeth," sniped Alice caustically.

"Gee thanks. You're looking gorgeous too—have you had your feathers done?" retorted Elizabeth.

"The both of you look like you've been to pretty school," said Hannah snidely.

The insults continued until Elizabeth squawked, "there they are."

"They're awfully small," complained Hannah.

"Yeah," moaned Alice. "You got us out of our cozy nest for these pathetic little things."

The Harpies circled high above.

"But we need to kill them," crowed Elizabeth. "That's the rules."

"What rules?" asked Alice.

"What rules?" squawked Elizabeth. "You mean to tell me you haven't read the rules!"

"Of course I've read the rules," said Alice. "I just don't remember doing so."

"Well the rules say that if we ever spot a group of three strange little pretty things walking across our land we must kill them," said Elizabeth.

"Oh well, rules are rules," said Hannah. "Let's get it over with."

"But let's make it fun," said Alice.

Have you ever been really surprised? I don't mean a surprise-birthday-party sort of surprise that you've known about for weeks. What I mean is the sort of surprise you get when you're lying in bed reading a book and a ghost suddenly appears and vacuums your carpet. A real startling-unexpected-shocking-disquieting-surprise. Well that's the sort of surprise Simon, Ross and Melissa got when the Harpies attacked. You'd think that as they were on an island full of mythological monsters nothing could surprise them. But it did. You'd think that they would have been on constant lookout for creatures that might kill them. But they weren't. You'd think that they would have kept themselves hidden. But they hadn't.

No—the Harpies took them by startling-unexpected-shocking-disquieting-surprise.

The children had stopped for lunch at a shady spot close to the beach. It was a beautiful sunny day—the type of day that's perfect for lazing by the sea—and they were wishing they could stay there rather than have all the bother of saving the world from Doctor X.

As silently and secretly as feathers floating in a flurry of snow the Harpies moved in. They landed on rocks close to the children. Apart from some hissing from Melissa's snakes their arrival went unnoticed.

With a nod from Elizabeth all three Harpies suddenly shouted, "Boooo."

Actually they shouted, "λπκόόόό" which is Ancient Greek for "Boooo" but, as it sounds exactly the same as "Boooo," it had the very same effect.

Startled, the children jumped up screaming. When they saw how grotesquely ugly the Harpies were they screamed again. When they realized they were surrounded by three of these massive killer birds with no hope of escape they screamed again, only louder and with more conviction.

"Ooops," said Alice. "I do believe we've given the silly little things a fright."

"Yeah and they make an awful lot of noise for their smallness," said Hannah.

"Poor little beasties," said Elizabeth.

Elizabeth nodded again and, as if the three Harpies weren't frighteningly ugly enough, they started pulling scary faces.

Elizabeth gave a huge grin which not only showed her maggot ridden teeth but caused her huge purple tonsils to stick out of her mouth like a second tongue.

Alice puffed up her mouth causing her cheeks to swell so much that her warts squirted out a gooey green puss all over Simon. Hannah twisted her nose rapidly from side to side and made it pick putrid wax from her ears—which she then popped into her mouth and used to blow a giant bubble.

The children screamed again. Suddenly they realized that although screaming was a fairly normal reaction on seeing three disgustingly ugly Harpies making even uglier faces, it wasn't actually a very helpful response.

They ran!!!!

"Will we chase them?" asked Hannah.

"Nah," replied Elizabeth. "Give them a minute. Let them think they're escaping."

The children scurried from the beach and sprinted across a field towards the woods. Precisely one minute later the Harpies followed.

They had almost reached the cover of the trees when Alice swooped. She lashed out with her wart encrusted claws. Ross took a blow to the back of his head and fell to the ground. Simon and Melissa had reached the woods before they discovered what had happened. When they looked back they saw Ross lying motionless on the grass with the three Harpies sitting around him.

"What are we going to do?" screamed Melissa, not really expecting Simon to have an answer.

Quick as a flash Simon grabbed two thick branches from the

ground and handed one to Melissa.

"If they touch Ross I'll kill them," he bellowed.

"But we can't kill them," said Melissa.

"What?" said Simon.

"We can't kill them," repeated Melissa. "We don't know if they're villagers or animals. In fact they could easily be my mom, dad and sister."

"Well we have to rescue Ross," said Simon firmly. "I'll try not to harm them but if it's a choice between Ross and them you'll see a lot of feathers fly."

Melissa nodded slowly, fighting back her tears.

"Get them," yelled Simon.

"Try not to hurt them too much," pleaded Melissa.

They ran out from the bushes shrieking wild threats and frantically waving the branches. The Harpies hadn't expected this and, before they could take off, Simon and Melissa were whacking at their wings and legs.

"Ouch," exclaimed Alice. "You never told us they could sting."

"That's right," complained Hannah as the Harpies rose into the air, "you just said 'kill'—you never mentioned the bit about getting hurt."

"Don't be such wimps," squawked Elizabeth. "They're too small to really hurt us."

"Well," replied Alice indignantly. "I have a leg that would like to disagree with that."

"Oh bother," moaned Elizabeth. "Why's it always me that needs to do everything around here?"

Elizabeth swooped down again and grabbed Melissa in her huge talons.

"Come little one," cooed Elizabeth. "Come to mommy."

CHAPTER 19
Melissa gets a wriggly snack and almost gives it back

"Get her worms, you useless cretins," squawked Elizabeth. Moaning as they went, Alice and Hannah flew from the nest.

"There's a good little thing," crowed Elizabeth with a coochy-coo sort of voice. "Mommy will look after you."

Melissa struggled to free herself but her legs and lower body were firmly trapped beneath the foul smelling Harpy like a little chick under a big fat mother hen. She gripped onto a branch of the nest and pulled with all her strength but it was hopeless, she couldn't move an inch.

Alice and Hannah arrived back, wriggly things dangling from their mouths.

"Din dins," said Elizabeth, forcing a couple of big juicy worms into Melissa's mouth.

The worms wriggled and tickled. Melissa felt sick.

"Come on. Swallow," said Elizabeth whacking Melissa on the head. This caused Melissa to gulp and the worms slithered down her throat.

"Good girl," squawked Elizabeth. "That was very clever."

Melissa screwed up her face in utter disgust.

"Isn't she cute?" said Elizabeth.

"Yuck," replied Hannah noncommittally.

"You know, she's just like the baby I never had and never wanted," said Elizabeth.

"Mmmmm," said Alice feeling revolted at having this sweet little beast in her nest.

"So cute," said Elizabeth. "So very, very cute."

Elizabeth gave Melissa a little kiss.

"What do you think girls," continued Elizabeth. "Isn't she the prettiest little bundle of joy you've ever seen?"

"Stop being such a big softy," said Hannah abruptly. "You can't keep her."

"No it wouldn't be right," agreed Alice.

"Keep her!" exclaimed Elizabeth. "Why would we keep her? No we're going to tear her limb from limb."

CHAPTER 20
Me's burnt me's dinner

"Why's me's dinner up a tree?" asked the Eagle Head.

"Because," said the Wolf Head.

"Because what?" asked the Eagle Head.

"Just because," said the Wolf Head.

"Me's want me's dinner now!" said the Eagle Head.

"So what are we going to do?" said the Goat Head, looking at the Wolf Head.

"Same as we always do when our prey gets stuck up a tree," replied the Wolf Head.

"Starve?" said the Goat Head.

"No—burn it down," said the Wolf Head.

"Oh that," said the Goat Head.

"Me's still hungry," said the Eagle Head.

Mr. McRoast's three heads breathed flames onto the tree. The bark caught fire. Clouds of black smoke rose into the air.

CHAPTER 21
Not surprisingly Simon and Ross are surprised

Simon and Ross had tried to follow the Harpies but soon lost sight of them. Exhausted and worried they were now becoming desperate. They'd been searching for over two hours without spotting Melissa's kidnappers and had lost all sense of where they were and where they had already looked. They knew that without Melissa they wouldn't be able to find Doctor X and stop him taking over the world. They panicked. Then, in the distance, they saw smoke rising. Panic changed to surprise. Surprise gave way to fear. Fear turned to panic with just a hint of surprise. They ran towards the smoke hoping that it would lead them to Melissa. They hoped that she wasn't being roasted on some weird creature's barbeque.

CHAPTER 22
Me's out of here

"What's that black stuff coming into our nest?" squawked Elizabeth.

"It looks like little black clouds that have got lost," said Alice.

"Do go and take a proper look," commanded Elizabeth.

"Why do we have to do all the hard work?" moaned Alice.

"I'm busy looking after the baby aren't I?" snapped Elizabeth.

Alice and Hannah flew out of the nest and reluctantly took a proper look.

"Oh dear," said Hannah. "Oh dear, oh dear, oh dear."

"What's up?" crowed Elizabeth.

"There's a funny creature at the bottom of our tree," replied Hannah. "We seem to be having a plague of them today."

"Should we kill it?" asked Alice.

"Dunno," replied Elizabeth. "We've still got this pretty little one to kill."

"I think this one is causing the black clouds," said Hannah.

"Yeah, let's kill it," said Alice. "I don't like the look of it."

"Okay," said Elizabeth. "If you want."

The three Harpies flew down from the top of the tree.

With all three heads Mr. McRoast took one look at the vile creatures plunging towards him and fled as fast as his four legs would carry him.

The flames rose up towards Melissa.

CHAPTER 23
Melissa discovers that what goes up must come down

As Simon and Ross neared the burning tree they realized Melissa was stuck at the very top. This wasn't due to any special powers of observation—it was more to do with the fact that she was emitting tonsil tearing screams.

"You'll have to climb down as far as possible and jump the rest," instructed Simon.

"I can't," sobbed Melissa.

"You must," said Simon.

"I'm afraid of heights. I can't climb trees," said Melissa.

"You've got to try," said Simon. "I'll guide you down."

"I'm scared," said Melissa.

"Crawl to the edge of the nest and grab hold of a thick branch," commanded Simon.

Nervously Melissa edged her way across the nest. Beneath her the flames grew higher. Cautiously she stretched out and grasped the edge. As she did, the branch decided that it had had enough of supporting the weight of a huge nest, and assorted creatures—it snapped. The nest and Melissa tumbled through the air, crashing to the ground beside the boys.

"Well done," said Simon. "You made it."

CHAPTER 24
Finding a nine-headed creature in the marsh
gives the children a sinking feeling

Eager to get as far away as possible from the Harpies the children walked until the sun had set and darkness was closing in. When they were too exhausted to go further they flopped down beneath a large rowan tree and immediately fell asleep.

Melissa dreamt that she and her sister Amanda were making perfume from rose petals borrowed from a neighbor's bushes then selling it on eBay for a vast profit.

In Ross's dream he was playing the world chess champion, Brian Rookcastle and had a forced checkmate in fourteen moves. In a few moments he'd be crowned the youngest ever king of the chess world.

Simon dreamt that his mother's pink-leather sofa had grown pink-leather wings and was chasing him around the park. His mother was sitting on it shooting arrows at him from a little pink bow while she watched television.

The children woke later than they'd intended. After an energizing breakfast of potato chips and fizzy orange juice, they set off again. As they approached the north of the island the woods thinned out. The few trees that managed to grow there were stumpy and leaned southwards. After another couple of miles there were no trees at all. Here the land was constantly beaten by a northerly wind and no plants of height could withstand its power. Even during summer high winds strong enough to carry a person away often sprung up out of nowhere. This was the marshlands—the no-go area of the island. There were no sheep or cattle farmed here. Even the wild animals such as deer and fox kept well clear. For the next few miles the land was covered in heather but eventually even this became sparse. The ground turned wet and boggy. Every footstep sank into peaty soil and progress became slow and painful. Each time they thought they'd found a route through the marsh they'd come to a stretch of water too deep to cross and would have to turn back.

"Is there no other way?" moaned Ross.

"Sure," said Melissa. "We could go back and face those ugly birds again then get lost trying to find our way across the island."

Simon looked at his Ultra-Accurate-Atomic-Wrist-Watch. "We've only gone about a mile in the last three hours. This is a huge waste of time."

"Fine," said Melissa, her snakes spitting venom, "you find a better route."

"Look, cool it," said Simon, recoiling from the hissing snakes. "I'm not saying I know a better route. All I'm saying is that this way is dreadfully slow and there's nowhere to hide if we're spotted by another killer creature."

"How much further does this marsh go on for?" asked Ross.

"I've no idea," confessed Melissa, "it could be miles."

Simon wanted to yell at Melissa for not knowing the island she lived on, but he bit his tongue. They continued in scornful silence.

It was perhaps fortunate that they walked in silence. It certainly was fortunate that they were going slowly. Otherwise they'd have walked straight into the marsh creature's lair. But they didn't. It was Ross who spotted it. At first he thought it was just his imagination or perhaps the wind blowing on a clump of heather. Something was moving on the marsh. Ross whispered to the others. They stopped and stared. For a while nothing happened. Then Melissa glimpsed something rise out of the marsh. She pointed. About two-hundred yards in front of them was some sort of creature. A large snake-like head became clear. Slowly it raised itself higher and higher on a long scaly neck. Another head appeared and then another and another.

"There are six of them," whispered Melissa.

"No eight," whispered Ross.

"There's at least nine," said Simon, as the final head appeared.

A massive serpent body lifted itself from the murky water and there before them was the largest creature any of them had ever seen. Instinctively they turned to run. But the cruel marsh held them fast.

The creature was a Nine-Headed-Hydra though previously it had been Ben Cattlegrid the rather eccentric farmer who owned most of the east of the island. To say that a Nine-Headed-Hydra is big is a bit like calling a blue whale a cute little goldfish. A Nine-Headed-Hydra is in fact extraordinarily, massively, hugely gigantic with a little bit added on. Its body looks like an overgrown dragon, with rough scaly skin and a long spiky tail. At the other end, of course, are its nine heads. Each of these has an immense horn sharp enough to rip open a submarine and a mouth full of flesh-shredding teeth. Should any of its heads be knocked off in battle the Hydra simply grew a new one—a useful feature when there's a lot of fighting to be done.

In his new form Ben was rather proud of having more heads than any other creature on the island. Before his transformation he had been very proud of having the biggest collection of used tractor tires on the island (he had 1,742). Although Ben's heads were filled with memories of what happened during ancient times, sadly he had no memory of the used tractor tires or indeed anything about himself before he was transformed into the Nine-Headed-Hydra. This was such a pity for he would have been doubly proud at having the most used tractor tires and the most heads on the island. It was perhaps Ben's eccentric personality being carried over into his new body that caused the Nine-Headed-Hydra to move far away from the village and set up home in the remote, lonely wind swept marsh.

"Okay, keep calm," whispered Simon. "The trick is not to panic."

Running through the marsh was impossible but with a huge nine-headed beast so close every nerve in their bodies said "RUN"—in block capital letters.

"We need to move slowly and carefully," Simon continued. "If we do that we'll get away without it seeing us."

Ross tried to make a witty reply about never running away from a marsh monster unless it gives you a nine-head start but he was so scared that when he spoke he talked gibberish.

The children held hands to reduce their chances of falling and slowly began to shuffle away from the beast. Had they looked back they may have discovered that the Nine-Headed-Hydra couldn't see them. No—in fact, just like Ben, the creature was short sighted. Actually it was busy searching for a rock it had dropped in the marsh the previous day—one of a collection it was making in an attempt to become the creature with the biggest rock collection on the island.

But the children did hear it speak. They heard the words, "Trying to find a rock in this marsh is like trying to find a tractor tire in a haystack" drift across the marsh. But this seemed such a bizarre thing for anyone to say that they decided the noise was just the wind.

They kept going until they were back at the start of the marsh. Too tired to even find a bush to hide under they threw themselves to the ground and fell asleep.

CHAPTER 25
The wood nymph, Echo, makes Melissa
do the Highland Fling—badly

Melissa woke up, stretched and yawned. It was early morning. The sun shone brightly, creating little rainbows of color as it struck the dew that perched in little globules upon the heather. Melissa lay still—her legs stiff and aching. Her snakes were restless and were the reason she awoke so early. They were stretching out in the direction of the marsh, hissing angrily. Peering out through sleepy eyes, Melissa saw a beautiful young girl skipping and dancing across the marsh. Her feet skimmed the surface as if she was weightless. For a few minutes Melissa watched in stunned amazement while the girl danced and sang a cheerful little song.

> Tra la la,
> Diddle le de de
> Dancing on water

With a song full of glee
Nothing brings more joy
To king or to tree
Than watching the dance
Of beautiful me.
Beautiful me, beautiful me.

The girl smiled a beamingly happy smile. She'd spotted Melissa watching and was delighted to have an audience. Still skipping and dancing she hurried towards Melissa. Melissa shook Simon and Ross but by the time they were awake the young girl was standing beside them.

"Hello," she said all bubbly and joyful. "I'm Echo. Oh, it's so good to meet you. There are very few people on this island. In fact I don't think I've seen any since I got here—apart from you of course." Turning to Melissa she continued, "Did you enjoy my dancing? Good. I knew you would. I really am extremely gifted, even if I say so myself—which I do. But many other people have complimented me on my wonderful dancing and singing. In fact only last week I was dancing for King Allthingsbrightandbeautiful and do you know what he said? No of course you don't—you weren't there. Well he said to me, 'Echo your dancing is sublime. You are more nimble than the moonlight itself. In fact you're an even more beautiful dancer than the fairy Princess Lightasafeatherandsoftonhertoes.' Now that was a wonderful thing for him to say don't you think?"

"Yes," said Melissa, "you do dance well."

"Thank you," said the girl, smiling gleefully. "You are very kind to say so. When next I meet the King I will certainly tell him what you said. I could teach you some of my special dances if you wish. Would you like me to dance for you again? Yes of course you would."

Before anyone could speak the little girl was performing the most stunningly amazing ballet dance across the marsh.

"Who's that?" said Simon.

"I've no idea," said Melissa.

"Is she from the island?" said Simon.

"I don't think so. I've never seen her before," said Melissa.

"Haven't you noticed something strange about her?" said Ross.

"Yes, she dances across the marsh as if it was solid ground," said Melissa.

"Yeah," said Ross, "and she has little wings."

"Wow!" said Melissa. "I hadn't noticed that."

"So she must be one of Doctor X's creatures," said Simon. "We need to be very careful."

Simon got no prizes for guessing correctly—for of course the little girl was one of Doctor X's creations. Previously she'd been Melissa's cat, Snowy. Now she was a beautiful young wood nymph with a wonderful talent for dancing. There was another strange thing about her—apart from having wings and being able to dance on water. Unlike most of the other creatures on the island she could speak English. And, since she had previously been a cat, this was even more remarkable. Isn't Doctor X's scigic amazing? By changing the DNA of animals and humans not only could he create strange creatures with nine heads but he could give cats the ability to speak English! Wow!! I wish I could do that—I'd turn my best friend into a talking frog. Sadly all my attempts to change him have failed miserably—but I'll keep trying.

"There, did you enjoy that as much as me? I'm sure you did," said Echo when she finally stopped dancing. "But why are none of you smiling? You all look so sad. Oh, I've just realized that you haven't told me your names. I could guess them of course but that may take a while. Now you know that I'm Echo because I told you so. Well originally I came from a wonderful village called Toadstool by the Lilly Pond. But that was a long time ago and I've traveled to so many fabulous places since then. Isn't this a beautiful island? Have you seen the sea? It's such a lovely shade of blue when the sun is shining on it. I just wish there were more people on the island that I could dance for . . ."

"My name is Simon," interrupted Simon, "these are my friends Ross and Melissa."

"Nice to meet you I must say," said Echo. "I do love your hair Melissa—snakes are so modern." Giving a twirl she continued, "Do you like my dress? It's made from butterfly and dragonfly wings. Princess Versacedesignerclothesfortheveryrich created it especially for me when I was to perform a ballet for Queen Drinkstoomuchelderberrywine. Isn't it just the prettiest thing you have ever seen?"

She twirled again so everyone could get another look. Simon glanced at his watch. "Gosh," he said. "Look at the time. It's been nice meeting you but we really must go now."

"Go?" said Echo with a grin. "Oh you can't go—and anyway it's still early. There's such a lot of dancing to be done. Please stay and dance with me. We'll have such fun together. Come let me show you how to . . . "

"No," said Simon forcefully. "We have to go now."

"Go if you must," said Echo, still smiling. "But you'll miss my best dances. Tell me—where are you going in such a hurry that you can't stay to watch a dance or two? What could possibly be so important that you can't stop a short while?"

"We're going to the north of the island," said Simon, not wishing to tell this strange little girl any more than necessary.

"To the north!" exclaimed Echo and laughed. "You can't possibly attempt to cross the marsh to go north. Don't you know about the marsh monster? Don't you know that he'll eat you all up? Silly things—you'll never cross the marsh unless you know the secret route."

"Secret route," said Melissa. "What secret route?"

"The marsh is a labyrinth of paths. Some are easy, some are difficult, most are impossible. But they all lead to one place—the monster's lair. All except one. One secret path takes you to the north without the inconvenience of being eaten by the monster."

"Do you know the path?" asked Melissa.

"Of course I do. I know everything about the marsh. I have danced across it ten thousand times. What do you think of the heather? Isn't it the most incredible shade of purple you have ever seen? Once, after dancing for the King, I received a bouquet of flowers and they were exactly the same . . ."

"Echo," interrupted Melissa. "Please tell us where the path is."

"Tell you? I can't possibly do that," said Echo with a laugh. "I can't tell you, for the path changes constantly. If I told you where the path is now, it would be different when you tried to cross. You need to find the path by instinct. It's like dancing; you can only really dance well if you dance by instinct. My mother told me that I danced from the moment I was born. I don't remember a single day that I haven't danced. Do you like dancing Melissa?"

"Yes I do," replied Melissa rather embarrassedly as this was a lie. "But right now we need your help. This is very important. Will you please guide us across the marsh?"

"Of course I will. You are my friends," said Echo with a beaming smile. "But first you must let me see you dance. Dance a wonderful dance for me and then I'll take you safely across the marsh."
Melissa turned bright red. About a year ago she'd started Highland Dance lessons but after four weeks she got bored and gave up. She'd been the worst dancer in the class and she could barely remember anything she'd learned.

"Oh I couldn't possibly dance without music," she said.

"Ross and I will hum for you," said Simon, pushing Melissa forward.

"I'm not sure that I can dance right now," said Melissa. "My legs are very tired."

Simon nudged her hard in the ribs.

"Dance!" he commanded.

Melissa walked a short distance from the group. While Simon and Ross hummed the tune of 'Scotland the Brave' Melissa tried her best to do the Highland Fling but she stumbled and fumbled, she flopped when she should have flung and she skirled when she should have twirled.

Echo cheered enthusiastically and, when Melissa had finished, she clapped with great excitement.

"That was wonderful," she exclaimed. "I've never seen dancing like that before. It's strange but I love it. Dance for me again. Dance Melissa."

Melissa danced—reluctantly. Then, at Echo's request, she danced again and again and again. Eventually Simon intervened.

"That's enough dancing," he commanded. "Now Echo take us across the marsh as you promised."

"Okay," said Echo. But for the first time she spoke without smiling.

CHAPTER 26
The children cause the Nine-Headed-Hydra a dining dilemma

E cho danced her way across the marsh with the children following close behind.

"Dance. Dance. Dance," she sang merrily, as she zigzagged to and fro. "The only way to see the path is to dance."

They moved more quickly now. This route was easier. Their feet didn't sink into the soggy marsh so much and their legs didn't ache quite as badly as they had the day before.

When she wasn't singing Echo talked non-stop—mainly about what a wonderful dancer she was and how she'd danced for kings and queens and princes and princesses. At times Simon wanted to strangle her for talking so much but he had no choice but to put up with her.

"Here we are," she sang sweetly.

"This can't be the north of the island." said Simon, "We're nowhere near the sea."

But Echo didn't reply. Instead she vanished.

"Where's she gone?" said Melissa.

They looked all around. In every direction the land was flat and barren for miles. There was nowhere for Echo to hide yet there was no sign of her.

"She's tricked us!" said Simon.

"We were stupid to trust her," said Melissa.

"Where are we?" asked Ross.

"Looks like we're in the very middle of the marsh," said

Simon.

"I think we're in great danger," said Melissa, stroking her snakes to calm them.

"We're probably not far from that monster," said Simon.

"So what are we going to do?" said Ross.

"We could catch the next helicopter out of here?" said Simon, in the sarcastic voice he normally reserved for answering his history teacher.

Before they could do anything they heard a loud 'gluurrrrp' as a large scaly head lifted itself out of the marsh.

"Dear me," it said, "where did I put that nice rock?"

There was another 'gluurrrrp' and a second head appeared.

"Any sign of it, Number Six?" it asked.

"No, Number Four," replied Number Six. "I seem to have lost it."

'Gluurrrrp', 'gluurrrrp', 'gluurrrrp'. Another three heads popped up from the marsh.

"We'll never have the biggest rock collection on the island if you keep losing them Number Six," said Number Nine.

"Sorry," said Number Six.

"Sometimes sorry is just not good enough," said Number One.

'Gluurrrrp', 'gluurrrrp', 'gluurrrrp', 'gluurrrrp'. All nine heads were now stretching out of the marsh, supported by nine long reptile necks.

"Look," said Number Four, blinking to clear the mud from his eyes. "There are three rocks over there."

Heads Two, Six and Seven stretched out and grabbed the objects.

"Ooooh," spluttered Number Two, in a gargled voice, due to the fact that he had Ross in his mouth. "This is a very strange rock. It's soft."

"There's no such thing as a soft rock you numbskull," said Number Three.

"That's right," said Number Eight. "If it's not hard then it's not a rock."

"Well mine is soft too," slurped Number Six.

"Nonsense," said Number Nine. "Let me see one of them." Head Number Nine shook the watery mud out of his eyes and blinked a few times before moving close to Head Number Two.

"That's not a rock," he pronounced. "That's a thingy."

"A thingy!" said Number's Three, Five and Seven in unison. "What's a thingy?"

"You know," said Number Nine. "One of those thingy things . . . a whatchamacallit."

"Never heard of a whatchamacallit," spluttered Number Six with a mouthful of Simon.

"Yes you have," said Number Nine. "You ate one last week."

"A Roman Warrior?" spluttered Number Six. "Are you telling me that I have a Roman Warrior in my mouth?"

"No. Not a warrior," said Number Nine. "The same only smaller."

"Oh, an Egyptian Princess," suggested Number Four.

"No, smaller still," said Number Nine.

"He means a child," spluttered Number Seven.

"That's it," said Number Nine. "It's a child—not a rock."

"Well that's no use," said Number One.

"Unless we try to make the biggest collection of children on the island," suggested Number Five.

"Why would be want to do that?" asked Number Eight sarcastically.

"Just a suggestion," sniffed Number Five.

"Well what are we going to do with them?" spluttered Number Two.

"Don't quite know," said Number Nine. "What can you do with children?"

There was a short silence as the heads gave some serious

thought to this dilemma.

"Do they bounce?" asked Number Eight. "I like things that bounce."

"No," said Number Three. "You're thinking of coconuts. They bounce."

"Coconuts crack," said Number Four. "They don't bounce."

"Why don't you let us go?" said Melissa, suddenly plucking up the courage to speak.

"Ooooo," said Number Eight. "They talk."

"That's it," spluttered Number Seven. "Children talk—that's what they do."

"Please let us go," said Melissa.

"Let them go," said Number Nine. "Now there's something we hadn't thought of. We could let them go."

"Would that be fun?" asked Number One.

"Don't know," replied Number Nine. "But at least it's something we can do."

"Let's vote on it," said Number Four. "Who says we let them go?"

"Me," said Number Eight.

"Me too," spluttered Number Two.

"And me," said Number Nine.

"Me," said Number Three.

There was a long period of silence as the children's fate hung in the balance.

"Well . . . " said Number One very slowly, "okay . . . me too."

"Right. Decision made," said Number Nine, "we let them go."

Heads Two, Six and Seven began lowering the children to the ground.

"Wait a minute," slurped Number Six, with a sudden rush of enthusiasm, "I've just remembered . . . children . . . we eat children . . . that's what we do with them."

"Eat them!" said Number nine. "Are you sure?"

"Yes," slurped Number Six. "They have a sweet peppermint taste with just a hint of wild berries."

"Mmmm," said Number Nine, licking his lips. "I like the sound of that."

"So are we going to eat them or not?" spluttered Number Seven.

"Yes," said Number Nine. "I guess that's the right thing to do."

"So can I start eating mine?" slurped Number Six.

"Don't see why not," said Number Nine.

"That's not fair," said Number Four huffily. "He got to eat the Roman Warrior last week."

"So?" spluttered Number Six.

"So I should get a turn," said Number Four.

"Well there are nine of us and only three children," said Number Nine. "So we need to decide who eats them."

"I want to eat mine," spluttered Number Six.

"And I want to eat mine," spluttered Number Two.

"Me too," slurped Number Seven.

"Hold on," said Number Four. "It was me that found them."

"But you thought they were rocks," spluttered Number Seven.

"So what?" said Number Four.

"Can I make a suggestion?" said Ross.

"Oooooh," said Number Three. "One of the children wants to make a suggestion."

"Cheeky thing," said Number Five.

"Let it speak," said Number Nine. "Let's hear what it has to say."

"Why not have a contest?" said Ross. "Whoever wins decides which heads get to eat us."

"That's brilliant," exclaimed Number Nine. "Wish I'd thought of that."

"I thought of it," said Number Five. "I just didn't say."

"Sure!" said Number Three.

"What sort of contest?" asked Number Nine.

"I'll set you a riddle," said Ross.

"Excellent," said Number Nine. "And the winner decides who eats these very nice children."

CHAPTER 27
Ross sets a riddle to checkmate the Nine-Headed-Hydra

Ross searched his memory for the hardest chess riddle he could think of. This wasn't easy to do while being held in the grip of head Number Two of a Nine-Headed-Hydra—especially since its teeth were jagging into his ribs. Ross loved everything to do with chess. At home he spent hours solving complicated chess puzzles. He believed that that was why he was Scottish Junior Champion and why one day he would become a chess grand master (if they managed to get to Doctor X and persuade him not to take over the world and if he studied hard at school and got into university and also, of course, as long as he ate all his greens.) Finally Ross settled on a riddle he'd thought up a few months ago—it had bamboozled all his friends at the chess club. He cleared his throat.

"In a chess game, what's the fewest number of moves a pawn must make to return to the position it started in?" he asked nervously.

"Oooowww," exclaimed, Number Nine. "A chess riddle. I love chess."

"Don't be silly," said Number One. "You can't play chess."

"Yes I can," protested Number Nine. "I was playing it just last month."

"That was football," said Number One. "And you're rubbish at that as well."

"Can we concentrate on the puzzle?" spluttered Number Six.

"It's hard enough trying to think with a delicious child in my mouth without listening to you as well."

"Ooohhh," said Number One sarcastically. "Excuse me for existing."

"A pawn can't get back to its own square," said Number Four. "For it can never move backwards."

"It must be able to get back somehow or there'd be no riddle," spluttered Number Two.

"I've got it. I've got it," said Number Three. "When the game is over, it will be put back on its own square ready for the next game. So it's the fewest number of moves to complete a game."

"That can't be the answer," spluttered Number Seven.

"Yes it can," said Number Three.

"It was a good try," said Ross. "But I'm afraid it's the wrong answer. The pawn must get back to its own square legally during the game."

"Twenty-three moves," said Number Eight.

"Twenty-three!" exclaimed Number One. "How did you get twenty-three?"

"Worked it out," said Number Eight.

"No you didn't," said Number One.

"Did," said Number Eight.

"No you didn't. You just guessed a number. You're hopeless," said Number One.

"Bet I'm right," said Number Eight.

"Bet you're not," said Number One.

"Double bet," said Number Eight.

"So is he right?" asked Number One, prodding Ross in the stomach.

"Sorry," said Ross. "It's not the right answer.

"Okay," said Number Nine. "Everyone stop guessing and try and work this out logically."

"That's easy for you to say," spluttered Number Seven. "You

don't have a child stuffed in your mouth. Do you know how difficult it is to think without swallowing a tasty child that's in your mouth?"

"That's right," slurped Number Two. "We're at a great disadvantage."

"Yeah," agreed Number Six. "My mouth's watering constantly. All I can think about is eating."

"Why don't you put us down," said Ross.

"Put them down," said Number Nine. "Now that's a very good idea."

"Yeah," agreed Number Two. "Then we can think without wanting to chew."

"Right," said Number Nine. "It's agreed. Heads Two, Six and Seven-put them down."

"Wait," said Number Eight. "If we put them down they'll run away."

"Not if we promise not to," said Ross.

"Hah. You hadn't thought of that had you Number Eight?" said Number Nine.

"Well . . . " said Number Eight slowly. "Well . . . I guess that's okay."

"Right children," said Number Nine. "I want you to promise not to run away if we put you down."

"We promise," said Simon, Ross and Melissa.

"Cross my heart and hope to die," added Simon.

"Put them down and let's get on with the riddle," commanded Number Nine.

Heads Two, Six and Seven gently lowered the children to the ground.

"What if the pawn is captured?" asked Number Three.

"If it's captured it's dead, Stupid," said Number One. "No pawn ever escapes after it's captured."

CHAPTER 28
The children break their promise and make a break for freedom

"**W**alk slowly as fast as you can," said Simon. Ross and Melissa knew exactly what he meant. They had to get as far away from the Nine-Headed-Hydra as quickly as they could without him spotting them trying to escape. They headed towards the north but were soon knee high in muddy water and forced to change direction. That route was blocked too. Before they knew what was happening they were heading back towards the Hydra. The heads were still absorbed in the riddle so fortunately the monster didn't spot them even though they came within its limited range of vision.

"This is hopeless," whispered Simon. "All roads lead to Doom."

"All except one," said Ross. "Remember Echo said that one path leads to safety."

"Oh great. Well phone her up and ask her which one it is," snapped Simon.

"Dance!" exclaimed Melissa with a shriek of excitement. "She said dance and you'll see the secret route."

"Dance," said Simon, trying his best not to scream. "Cancel that order Ross. Don't phone Echo. Phone the Russian State Ballet and ask them if they could help us get out of a swamp."

"Don't be like that," said Melissa.

"Like what?" snarled Simon. "We're stuck in the mud with a lunatic monster and all you can suggest is dancing."

"Okay smarty-pants," said Melissa. "You come up with something better."

Simon fell silent. He had no idea what to do. And he absolutely hated not knowing what to do. Even more than that, he hated having to admit that he didn't know what to do.

"Let's give it a try," said Ross, breaking the tension. "We've got nothing to lose."

"Except our lives," said Simon under his breath.

"Everyone hum 'Flower of Scotland,'" said Melissa, "and dance as best you can."

They did. They hummed and danced their way slowly through the marsh.

"Thank goodness my friends are all statues," muttered Simon. "If they saw me doing this . . . "

But somehow dancing worked. Gradually the path became easier and they picked up speed. An hour later they'd left the marsh behind and were at the north of the island. By this time they were all feeling a lot less irritable.

"That was a smart move back there with that beast," said Simon, patting Ross on the back.

"Yeah," agreed Melissa. "But how did you know it would fall for your trick?"

"I couldn't be certain," replied Ross. "But when playing chess you need to be able to read your opponent and calculate whether he will fall for a gambit or trap. With that beast I just had the feeling I could trick it into letting us go."

"Brilliant," said Simon. "And I suppose I owe you an apology Melissa."

"Forget it," said Melissa. "It's been a tough day. Let's get some sleep."

CHAPTER 29
Hunger makes me's nose hurt

"M e's really, really, really, really, really hungry," said the Eagle Head.

"Shut up," said the Wolf Head.

"Well find me me's dinner," said the Eagle Head.

"Now we've picked up their scent we'll soon find them," said the Goat Head.

"Me's nose hurts cos me's hungry," said the Eagle Head.

"No," scowled the Wolf Head. "Your nose hurts because you keep breathing fire onto it."

"Me's do that when me's hungry," said the Eagle Head.

CHAPTER 30
Hamish the flying crocodile goes hunting

The children left the north of the island and began their journey down the west coast. The terrain changed dramatically once more. Twenty thousand years ago the whole island had been covered by a vast sheet of ice. As the ice melted and shifted it sculpted the landscape, creating Mount Taine and making the west coast rocky and hilly. From the sheer cliffs the Atlantic Ocean stretched out, separating Gogha from Canada by thousands of miles of hostile ocean. Along the coastline the occasional Silver Birch tree pushed up to blend in with the grays of the rocks. Small pockets of color were painted by the hardy bushes that defied the rocky soil.

The difficult terrain made walking slow and tiring but the children could see Mount Taine about fifteen miles ahead of them. Now they had a target——each step took them closer to their goal. Many of the small hills along the way were so steep they had to take rests to catch their breath.

"This is almost as slow as the marshes," panted Simon at the top of a particularly steep hill.

"Don't exaggerate," said Melissa.

"We're doing a good pace running down the hills," said Ross.

"But it feels as if all the up slopes are longer than the down slopes," said Simon.

The children each sat on a rock to rest.

"If we don't take too many breaks," said Simon, "we should reach the mountain by evening."

Ross and Melissa didn't reply—they knew that the chance of Simon letting them get any decent breaks was zero.

"Let's race to the bottom of the hill," said Simon after a few minutes.

Melissa was first to her feet, "Catch me if you can," she yelled.

Pushing and shoving each other, Simon and Ross set off after her as fast as their weary legs would carry them. But half way down Melissa tripped. It was this that started the strange sequence of events that followed. Melissa rolled over and over until she reached the bottom of the hill. The commotion frightened a wood pigeon that was feeding nearby. It rose into the sky, flying higher and higher. As Melissa lay on the ground moaning about her sore leg a golden eagle swooped across the sky and, with military precision, snatched the pigeon in steel-hard talons.

Even higher in the sky a weird creature hovered. Once Hamish Horseradish had been a chef at the island's only hotel, now he was a hungry bird. Hamish had been following the children for some time. He was not the precision killing machine that the golden eagle was. In fact heights made him dizzy and flying made him sick. But now his hunger was greater than his fear of flying. At the precise moment the eagle snatched the pigeon, Hamish launched his attack on the children. He plummeted from the clouds. Suddenly below him was the golden eagle. Quickly Hamish considered his options; snatch an easy meal out of the sky or dive bomb the children and risk splatting himself onto the ground. He chose the easier option.

With a few flaps of his powerful wings he slowed himself down. He hovered hesitantly alongside the eagle. The two birds stared at each other. The eagle panicked. It had never seen a flying crocodile before—in fact it had never seen any crocodile before. It stopped eating and dropped the remains of the pigeon. The headless body tumbled through the air and landed with a splat on Melissa's lap.

"Yuchhhhhh," screeched Melissa. "Yuchhhhhh and double yuchhhhhh."

While Melissa stared at the blood drenched carcass that lay on her skirt and screamed hysterically the boys looked to the skies. There was the majestic golden eagle. Staring it in the face was a sight that would have been funny if it were not so grotesque—a hungry crocodile with a toothy grin, supported in mid-air by large, scraggy black wings. Bewildered by this ugly Mona Lisa of the skies the eagle decided not to hang around. It flew off at speed. Hamish followed, snapping his teeth as he flew. The eagle was by far the faster of the two but, not being accustomed to being hunted it decided to attack instead of retreat. It about turned and flew at Hamish with the speed of a heat-seeking missile. Taken by surprise Hamish was too slow to respond and the eagle's talons ripped across one of his eyes. Blinded by blood Hamish tumbled earthwards. The eagle followed and struck him from above. Oily black feathers fluttered towards the ground. Shaken but not seriously hurt Hamish steadied himself. Now he was really angry as well as really hungry. He focused his mind on destroying his opponent. The eagle circled and prepared to go in for the kill. The mighty birds flew towards each other at ferocious speed. Sensing victory the eagle stretched out its flesh ripping claws to tear its enemy to pieces. But it hadn't realized just how large an opponent it was dealing with and, at the moment of impact, Hamish opened his huge jaws. The eagle flew straight into Hamish's mouth and was never seen again.

"Run," yelled Simon, suddenly realizing they could become the next course of Hamish's meal. They sprinted to a small clump of bushes and threw themselves to the ground. Unfortunately the area was covered in thistles that stung their legs, but the danger had passed. Hamish had had enough to eat and happily flew off for a post-lunch nap.

The children stayed where they were for some time to make sure that the flying crocodile had gone. Although no one would admit it, they were all pleased to have an excuse for a rest— especially Melissa whose ankle was still sore from her tumble. It made them realize how foolish they'd been running down the slopes for if any one of them broke a leg it would jeopardize their attempts to save the world from Doctor X. They agreed to slow down a little—although Simon did moan about wasting time.

A search in their backpacks revealed that all they had left were four bags of potato chips and three cans of fizzy cola. After eating a bag of chips each, they argued over who should have the very last one—a jumbo sized bag of 'Sweet and Sour Duck with Chive'. At last they resolved the dispute by drawing lots. Simon lost and was forced to eat the vile tasting chips. Luckily wild blueberries and raspberries grew on the island and, although these wouldn't be as enjoyable as potato chips and chocolate, at least they'd keep them from starving.

Many streams flowed from the mountain to the sea but the children were afraid the water may contain the scigic serum. So before drinking from any stream they waited until they saw a bird drink—for if the bird didn't turn into a monster then the water must be safe.

They continued on their journey and by late evening, exhausted and hungry, reached the foot of the mountain. Even on this side of the mountain Doctor X's land was protected by the electric fence. Simon and Ross threw stones at the electric wire that ran along the top. After a few good strikes the wire snapped allowing them to climb across without fear of electrocution. Once over the fence, Simon checked his Ultra-Accurate-Atomic-Wrist-Watch. "Let's climb for an hour before we rest for the night," he said.

I couldn't possibly repeat what Ross and Melissa said in reply but I can tell you that they did not travel further that day.

CHAPTER 31
The children get within a stone's throw of the flesh-hungry Mr. McRoast

During the night the temperature plummeted as winds, carried across the cold ocean, swept up the slopes of the mountain. Ross lay huddled up against a large rock too frightened to sleep and too frightened to stay awake. Beside him Simon let out a loud, irritating snore. Ross kicked him.

"Whaaaahh . . ." yelped Simon, "What's up?"

"I can't sleep," said Ross, "and when I do I have nightmares that some vile beast with six hideous heads is ripping us to bits and when I'm awake I worry that some vile beast with six hideous heads is about to rip us to bits."

"You try to sleep for a while," said Simon, "I'll keep guard."

"And I'm freezing," moaned Ross.

"Me too," said Simon. "Let's light a campfire."

There were very few broken branches lying around but eventually the boys gathered enough for a small fire.

"Let me light it," said Ross.

"It would be better if I lit it," said Simon.

"No, let me do it," said Ross. "At the Scouts I learnt how to start a fire by rubbing twigs together."

"If you insist," said Simon.

Ross rubbed and rubbed and rubbed until his hands ached but the twigs refused to produce even the hint of a spark.

"Stand back," said Simon, "Let an expert show you how it's done."

Simon moved close to the branches, shielding them from the wind. He unzipped his backpack and took out a box of matches. Seconds later the fire was burning and the boys began to feel warmer.

"You didn't tell me you'd brought matches," said Ross.

"You didn't ask," said Simon.

The boys sat talking for a long time until eventually they both dozed off.

When they awoke the fire had died out but, as the wind had dropped, it wasn't nearly so cold. Breakfast was little more than a few raspberries picked from bushes at the foot of the mountain. As they ate Melissa suddenly shrieked.

"Yuuuuck," she cried. "I've eaten a caterpillar."

"And you call yourself a vegetarian," teased Simon.

"What if it's not a caterpillar," she said, panicking. "What if it's one of Doctor X's creatures? What if I've just eaten my mom?"

"Did it have the head of a hideous hippopotamus?" joked Simon, finding Melissa's discomfort amusing.

"That's not funny," said Melissa fighting back her tears. "My parents could be any sort of weird creatures and we might never get back to normal."

"Don't worry," said Simon, "if you're stuck with those snakes you could become the biggest attraction the zoo has ever had."

Ross was more considerate. He searched the raspberry bushes and returned with a handful of caterpillars.

"They're not monsters," he said reassuringly. "They're just ordinary caterpillars—actually they're the young of the Meadow Brown butterfly."

Relieved that she hadn't eaten her mother, Melissa ate a few more berries—after washing them thoroughly in a nearby stream.

The mountain looked daunting. It was eighteen hundred feet high and strewn with large boulders that, over thousands of years, had broken off and rolled from the top. From the moment they set out Melissa's snakes were hyper-active and Simon and Ross kept a little distance from them—just in case. By taking a zig-zag route they avoided any seriously steep climbs. After five hours of scrambling they were about half way up, feeling smugly satisfied with their progress.

"Shhhh," whispered Ross. "I can hear talking."

"Yeah right," said Simon. "There's nobody on the mountain but us."

"I definitely heard a voice," insisted Ross.

"Voices in your head," mocked Simon.

"Someone said 'me's head hurts,'" replied Ross calmly.

"What!" said Simon. "Do you really think if a monster was about to kill us it would announce that it had a headache?"

Sixty feet further down the mountain the Wolf Head whispered, "Be quiet."

"But it does hurt," insisted the Eagle Head, rebelliously loudly. "There's a thunderstorm going on in my brain."

"I heard it again," whispered Ross. "It said something about thunder."

"How helpful," sniggered Simon. "We're half way up a mountain and someone is kind enough to give you a personalized weather forecast."

"I heard it too," whispered Melissa, "a squeaky little voice."

"That's right," said Ross.

"Okay. Okay," said Simon irritably. "Stay here while I go and check."

"No," said Melissa, blocking Simon's way. "We stick together."

"Well what would you suggest?" asked Simon.

"Let's go faster," said Ross nervously.

Even though every muscle in their legs ached, they somehow summoned up enough energy to raise their pace. Every so often Ross swung round in the hope of spotting the owner of the squeaky voice. But, although there was a clear view down the mountain, not even a bird was to be seen.

A short distance behind them Mr. McRoast moved invisibly from boulder to boulder following his prey.

"Me's eat now," said the Eagle Head.

"Not yet," said the Wolf Head. "Stalking is the best part of the kill. We strike when I say so."

"Now chill it," said the Goat Head.

Exhausted, the children reached the summit and took a well earned rest. Simon and Melissa were in jubilant mood, delighted at having conquered the mountain but Ross was subdued. Nightmares were still swirling around in his head. He was more convinced than ever that they were being followed. He scrambled along the ridge in an effort to spot their pursuer. After fifteen eye-straining minutes of searching he caught a glimpse of a creature scurrying amongst the rocks.

"Look," he whispered, pointing. "Something's down there."

"Where?" asked Melissa.

"It's behind that big rectangular rock," said Ross. "It looks like a wolf."

They stared down the mountainside.

"I can see it," said Melissa, after a few minutes. "It's just a goat."

"No, it's definitely a wolf," said Ross.

"Goat," insisted Melissa.

"Wolf," insisted Ross.

"Make up your minds," said Simon.

"Look," said Ross, as Mr. McRoast scrambled from one rock to another "There it is."

"It's got three heads," said Simon.

"They look really evil," said Melissa.

"Especially the wolf head," said Ross.

"That nasty beast would love to suck out your eyes," growled Simon, grabbing hold of Ross, "Then it would eat the rest of your body while you're not looking."

"I told you we were being followed," said Ross, pushing Simon away. "What are we going to do?"

"Hide," said Melissa.

"That's pointless," said Simon, "it's got our scent."

"Let's make a run for it," said Ross.

"We could never outrun that thing," said Melissa.

"We've got no choice," said Simon. "We have to fight."

He picked up two fist sized stones.

"Come on," he yelled eagerly as he threw them. "Let's get it."

Ross and Melissa picked up a few big stones and threw them at the three headed beast. Soon a flurry of stones were hurling towards it. The stones struck rocks and bounced and tumbled down the mountain.

"Me's not like all this noise," said the Eagle Head.

"Stop moaning," said the Goat Head.

"Dinner time," said the Wolf Head.

Mr. McRoast made a detour to avoid the hail of stones. Silently he bounded up the mountain and approached from the side. Melissa's snakes sensed danger. Annoyed that previous attempts to alert her had been ignored they took drastic action. They whacked her hard across her face, forcing her to look in the right direction. Melissa shouted a warning to the others. Simon was holding two massive stones. He took aim and threw the first. But it fell short of its target and bounced over Mr. McRoast's heads.

"Charge!" thought the Wolf Head.

The powerful beast surged forward and leapt into the air. Simon threw his second stone. It flew towards the beast. The beast soared towards the children. Stone and Eagle Head collided.

"Ouch," cried the Eagle Head. "Me's head hurts even more

now."

"Retreat," it thought.

"Get them," thought the Goat Head.

"Suck out their brains," thought the Wolf Head, licking his lips.

The great beast landed ten feet from the children. The body, receiving different signals from its heads, didn't know what to do. Ross grabbed the biggest stone he could find. Holding it in both hands he threw it with every last scrap of his energy. As if everything was happening in slow motion they watched the stone twist and turn in mid air as it rocketed towards the beast. It struck the Wolf and Goat Heads then thudded onto the huge Lion Body.

"Retreat," thought the Wolf Head.

"Thistles and Nettles," thought the Goat Head. (Which in Ancient Greek goat language were rather nasty swear words.)

"Me's famished," thought the Eagle Head.

Mr. McRoast slunk back down the mountain out of range of the stones. The children followed every movement as he crept slyly between the rocks. Again and again he came up the mountain but, whenever he got close, he was driven back with an onslaught of stones. But, no matter how hard they tried to chase him away, he wouldn't give up.

Simon looked at his Ultra-Accurate-Atomic-Wrist-Watch— two hours, twelve minutes and thirteen seconds had passed since they had first encountered the beast.

"This is wasting precious time," he said. "I hate wasting time. 'Look after the minutes and the hours will look after themselves,' is what I always say. But we're wasting much more than minutes."

"And it's getting dark," said Ross. "Then that thing will be able to sniff us out and we won't have a clue where it is."

"You're right," said Simon. "We need to do something soon or we're dead meat."

"Let's create an avalanche," said Ross.

"What?" said Simon.

"Most of the rocks on the mountain are loose. If we can get some rolling they'll hit others and soon we'll have a whole rock avalanche," said Ross.

"Brilliant!" exclaimed Simon.

"But that could kill the beast," said Melissa.

"Yes? . . . And? . . . " said Ross.

"And it might be my sister," said Melissa. "What if it is and we kill her?"

"What if the beast kills us?" said Ross, "Then who's going to stop Doctor X turning everyone into weird mythical creatures?"

"Isn't there something else we could do?" asked Melissa.

"Yeah sure," said Simon. "I'll go and ask it if it would mind not killing us until after we've saved the world."

A few minutes of stony silence passed before Melissa said quietly, "Okay let's do it—but only because we have no choice."

CHAPTER 32
In which the children rock the mountain to scare off Mr. McRoast

The children spent an age carefully planning the avalanche. Starting from the top of the mountain they worked out which rocks would be easiest to roll. They chose six each. Being the strongest and a show off Simon chose the biggest.

"Okay. Are you ready?" he yelled. "Let's rock and roll."
They pushed with all their might and three rocks tumbled down the mountain.

"Next," commanded Simon.

They scrambled to the next rocks and pushed. This process continued until each of them had started six rocks rolling. Some of the rocks rolled a short distance and ground to a halt. But, with the help of gravity, some gained momentum and smashed into other rocks, making them roll down the mountain too. Soon dozens of rocks were cascading down the mountainside.

Mr. McRoast was one hundred feet further down the slope planning his next attack when he heard the almighty rumble.

"What's that noise me's hears?" asked the Eagle Head.

"I think it's an earthquake," said the Wolf Head.

"No," said the Goat Head. "An earthquake sounds more like 'Zabooom Kapowwww'"

"An earthquake doesn't go 'Zabooom Kapowwww'—that's the noise a volcano makes," said the Wolf Head.

"Help!" yelped the Eagle Head. "The mountain's falling down!"

Suddenly all three heads realized that they were about to be crushed by a shower of rocks.

"Run," shrieked the Wolf Head.

"Thistles and Nettles," yelped the Goat Head.

"Me's wants me's mommy," cried the Eagle Head.

Mr. McRoast ran. He ran as fast as he could. Being an oversized lion this was pretty fast. But the rocks were moving faster. They were bouncing wildly down the mountain like huge balls and with each bounce they got nearer to Mr. McRoast. The leading rocks were almost upon him and behind rumbled hundreds more.

"What are we going to do?" asked the Wolf Head.

"What do we normally do when we're being chased by rocks?" said the Goat Head.

The Wolf Head searched his memory. "We've never been chased by rocks before," he said.

"Oh!" said the Goat Head.

"Me's thinks we's should hide behind that big, big, big rock," said the Eagle Head.

"That's stupid," said the Wolf Head, "You can't just hide from tumbling rocks."

"They're catching up on us," said Goat Head.

"We need a plan," said Wolf Head.

"But if we's were behind that big, big, big . . ." said the Eagle Head.

"Shut up!" interrupted the Goat Head.

"But . . ." said the Eagle Head.

"We don't need your silly opinion," mocked the Wolf Head, "What we need is . . ."

Before the Wolf Head could complete his sentence a huge rock struck the Lion Body. Mr. McRoast was thrown through the air. He hit the ground with a thud, rolling over and over. More rocks hit him making him spin faster. His body was tossed this way then that before plunging down a deep crevasse. Above him the rocks, carried by their momentum, flew over the crevasse. He lay dazed, sore, but safe in the little hollow. He stayed there, licking his wounds, until the last rock passed and the noise subsided.

"Well, shall we get on with our attack?" asked the Goat Head.

"Nah," replied the Wolf Head, "Those creatures are far too dangerous."

"Me's hungry," said the Eagle Head.

"Shut up," said the Wolf and Goat Heads in unison.

CHAPTER 33
Arguments in the night over what to do about Doctor X

S imon decided that they must travel through the night. He had
several reasons for this:

1) He was worried that the three headed lion might still be
following them.

2) If they didn't set out until morning it would be dark when
they reached the castle and a whole day would be lost.

3) Ross had insisted that they stop for the night.

Traveling down a mountain, through woods, in the dark holds
a vast number of dangers. There are lots of things to trip over like
tree roots, bushes and rocks. There are things to fall into like
streams and crevasses. In fact if your teacher tried to arrange this as
part of a school outing he would discover that it was forbidden
under rules 99i, 212z, 482h, 512l and 1274b-x. But Simon wasn't
caring about these dangers (or rules) he was worried about meeting
more of Doctor X's monsters and wanted to get to the castle as soon
as possible.

As they stumbled and fumbled their way through the darkness
they discussed what they should do about Doctor X.

"Let me talk to him and show him what a monster he's turned
me into," said Melissa. "I'm sure he'll see reason and reverse the
scigic."

"Yeah right," sneered Simon. "He's going to give up his plan to rule the world because of some snotty little girl with snakes in her hair."

"He might," said Melissa.

"Or he might turn Ross and me into oversized chickens and eat us for Sunday lunch," said Simon.

"Well, what's your brilliant plan?" said Melissa tetchily.

"Kill him," said Simon boldly. "The only safe mad-scientist-that-wants-to-rule-the-world is a dead one."

"Oh great! Fantastic!" scoffed Melissa. "And with Doctor X dead how are you going to reverse the scigic?"

Simon fell silent for a while—rethinking his plan.

"Okay," he said eventually. "We don't kill him—we torture him."

"No," said Ross. "Our only hope is to trick him."

"Trick him! How could we possibly trick him?" said Simon. "Oh, wait . . . I see it now . . . we say 'Right evil Doctor X, your card is the Ten of Diamonds and, by the way, we've made you accidentally turn all your monsters back into humans again.'"

"Not that sort of trick," snapped Ross.

"Well what kind of stupid trick are you thinking of?" sneered Simon.

"Torture and tricks won't work," said Melissa calmly. "Persuasion is our only hope with someone like Doctor X."

"Yeah gentle persuasion with the help of some thumb screws," said Simon.

The argument continued as they walked through the night and when they reached the castle grounds at dawn they still had no idea of how to deal with Doctor X. But they were exhausted and Simon agreed that they could have two hours sleep before entering the castle.

CHAPTER 34
Melissa meets her father but he strikes her
with a lightning bolt

The children slept for more than three hours. During a meager breakfast of berries and water Simon checked his Ultra-Accurate-Atomic-Wrist-Watch twenty two times and told Ross and Melissa to hurry up thirty three times. Still hungry they set out for the castle. Open lawns stretched from the woods to the entrance. Now all that separated them from their confrontation with Doctor X was one-hundred foot of grass. They stopped at the last of the trees and scanned for danger. The way seemed clear but a distant grunting sound grabbed their attention. From the far right of the castle a giant stomped into view. It trundled along a path at the side of the castle swinging its long arms back and forth. In one hand it held an oversized hammer which it thumped against the wall roaring, "έέλις α κή άτσφα". ("I hate this job.")

Another giant appeared from the opposite direction. The two met close to the castle door. Rather than give way, they pushed and kicked each other before stomping off. No sooner had these giants disappeared from sight than a third hobbled around from the far right corner of the castle. These were the three Cyclopes that grudgingly guarded the castle for Doctor X. Twice the size of a man these mean creatures would sooner bite off a baby's head than change its diaper. Their greenish bodies were covered in a mass of yellow wart-like lumps that made them look like they had some dreadful disease. Atop each of their massive bodies was a horned head with a single round eye right in the middle of the forehead.

These ill tempered creatures were Brontes, Argos and Steropes. Before they'd drunk Doctor X's serum Brontes had been a pet parrot called Satan, Argos was Mr. Porridge the librarian and Steropes, Melissa's father. Doctor X had forced them to guard the castle. For the past three days and nights they'd marched around it non-stop—without even a break to go to the restroom (so you can understand why they were extra, extra grumpy).

The Cyclopes argued about everything—sometimes they even argued about nothing. When put on guard duty they argued about which direction to walk while patrolling the castle. Even a fight didn't solve the disagreement and so Steropes and Argos go clock-wise while Brontes goes counter-clockwise. Each time they meet they fight rather than move out of each other's way.

After watching the Cyclopes for some time, Simon calculated that there was a period of twenty-one seconds while Brontes and Steropes were fighting when they could sneak past them and into the castle. They awaited the right opportunity. A few minutes later Brontes passed the entrance door just as Steropes was coming towards him.

"έφυγε Δεν λέξεις από την εξική," roared Brontes. ("Out of my way wartface.")

"αμβάνω Δεν βρθκ έηα έλέις," bellowed Steropes. ("No you

get out of my way you one-eyed freak.")

Steropes kicked Brontes in the stomach. Brontes retaliated with a strong uppercut. His hammer caught Steropes square on the chin. Steropes fell with a thud that shook the earth under the children's feet.

"Go for it!" shouted Simon.

They ran, reaching the door with nine seconds to spare. The two Cyclopes didn't see them; Steropes was picking himself up off the grass and Brontes was trudging away moaning about the weather.

"It's locked," yelled Simon as he pulled on the door handle.

"It can't be," said Melissa.

"It is," said Simon.

"Now what?" asked Ross.

Steropes was on his feet and approaching. He cursed when he spotted them pushing on the castle door. He hated children—even though he'd never seen one before. And the worst kind of children were the kind that tried to break into a castle he was protecting.

"αήθλια πα γα ικόττη ταΦ," he yelled in his grumpiest voice. (Which for legal reasons can't be translated into English.)

"Run!" shouted Simon.

They ran.

Steropes tried to run after them but, due to severe lumbago, he couldn't. This made him even grumpier.

"πο φολσ μέΦνο παό ενΩθ σιασό," he bellowed. ("Come back here please and let me snap your heads off.")

The children sprinted across the lawn towards the trees. Simon glanced back.

"The ugly big brute's too decrepit to chase us," he yelled, almost laughing.

Steropes hobbled slowly after them then stopped, for although he was lacking in intelligence, he knew he would never catch them. Grumbling he turned back to get on with his guard duties. Then, bit by bit, a piece of vital information filtered through from a part of his brain that he hadn't used for years.

"Ωέέέέέέ," he yelled as he remembered he had a special power—the power of lightning. With an inner sense of joy he raised his right hand, pointed his index finger and fired.

Zwwaaappppp.

An almighty flash lit up the sky. Melissa took the full blast. Hearing the thud Simon spun round. The lightning had temporarily blinded him but, through a haze, he could make out the outline of Melissa. She was lying motionless.

"Help," he yelled to Ross.

The boys grabbed Melissa by the arms and dragged her towards the trees.

With a huge grin painted across his face, Steropes raised his arm again.

Zzzwwaaarrppp.

The bolt of lightning sizzled past, just missing the boys' heads. It struck an ancient oak tree. The tree crashed to the ground a short distance ahead of them.

"Keep going," cried Simon.

Zwwaaaooffff. Zzzssooorrrppp. Steropes fired another two bolts. But they had reached the trees and were safe from his killer thunderbolts.

"Melissa. Melissa. Wake up Melissa!" shouted Simon.

But Melissa lay motionless—even her snakes seemed to have hissed their last hiss.

CHAPTER 35
*Getting to the castle with help from a friend
with an ugly crooked beak*

igh above the children, on a thick branch, sat a creature with large pink wings and an ugly crooked beak. She watched intently as Simon and Ross tried to convince Melissa that she was not dead. The creature leapt from the tree and clumsily hurtled towards them. She extended her claws in the vague hope of striking her target.

"Aaaaahhh!" screamed Melissa, coming out of her daze and seeing the vile bird about to crash into Ross.

Simon and Ross got such a fright at Melissa's scream they jumped back. The creature got a shock too, missed Ross and smashed into a tree trunk.

"Δεεν βρ ηέκ α έθν λέξ έ νθν εξις," she grumbled. ("Darn, I hate flying—I wish I was a fish or a rabbit or a nice little planet.")

The creature lay on her back flapping her wings in an effort to get up.

"Grab her!" yelled Melissa. "It's my friend. It's Jillian."

Nervously Simon and Ross pounced on the creature. They each grabbed a wing and pinned her firmly to the ground. Jillian tried to peck them with her razor sharp but ugly crooked beak. The boys ducked and dived to avoid injury.

"Stop that," commanded Melissa, standing over her friend.

"πίοοί ανηα ζή τη σηαζς για, " said Jillian. ("Who do you think you're talking to?")

"Jillian. It's me. It's Melissa. Your best friend," cried Melissa.

Jillian hissed violently and tried to strike Melissa with her ugly crooked beak.

"Listen to me," said Melissa. "We need your help."

Jillian struggled to get free. She lashed out mercilessly. Her ugly crooked beak sliced through Ross's skin. Blood poured down his right arm. He let go of her. With a powerful flap of her wings, she broke free from Simon and lifted from the ground.

"Don't let her get away," yelled Melissa.

"The beastly thing almost bit my arm off," said Ross.

"Don't be such a baby," said Simon.

Simon and Ross leapt at Jillian, grabbing hold of her back feathers. She flapped her wings frantically in an effort to escape but the boys dragged her back to the ground.

"Listen to me," pleaded Melissa. "Doctor X turned you into a horrid creature with an ugly crooked beak. You're really Jillian MacRaincoat-my best friend."

"ουσ ατμα οέστυσ υο τυασ," Jillian squawked. ("Friend? I wouldn't be seen dead with someone with snakes in her hair.")

"Please remember. Please Jillian," implored Melissa. "Remember me. We go to school together."

Jillian squawked even louder and struck out with her ugly crooked beak.

"And you have a dog called Iona," said Melissa. "Doctor X turned him into a monster too."

Jillian stopped struggling.

"βοβι βοβι ρέθ εβο ύση τεινα δικός ρέθ Δείτε επίσης," she said. ("Iona. Iona. I remember. I don't normally have wings. That's why it's so darn difficult to fly.")

"We need your help," said Melissa. "Do you understand?"

"δός ε διόκς θώ δι μδαοδυ φοίλφς φοοφ," said Jillian. ("I may be a bird with an ugly crooked beak but I'm not completely stupid.")

"We . . . need . . . your . . . help," said Melissa again only this time very slowly and very loudly.

"δός . . . ε . . . διόκς . . . θώ . . . δι . . . μδαοδυ . . . φοίλφς . . . . . . φοοφ," said Jillian again only this time very slowly and very loudly.

"If you understand what I'm saying nod your ugly crooked beak," said Melissa.

Jillian nodded her ugly crooked beak.

"You always were a great friend," said Melissa, stroking Jillian's feathers, "I've missed you so much."

"Σβ διπ ος φψ απ όκς," said Jillian (For goodness sake don't start getting all soppy.)

"Soon everything will be fixed out and we . . ." began Melissa.

"Oh come on," snapped Simon. "We don't have time for this."

Melissa gave Simon a dirty look then turned back to her friend.

"Jillian we need you to fly us to the castle," she said. "Can you do that?"

"ικ όδς ελδδ ησβού φί λούς να μυο υ ναέκ," said Jillian, ("I'll try but I'm not making promises—I can hardly fly ten foot without crashing") as she nodded her ugly crooked beak.

"Let her go," said Melissa.

"Are you sure?" said Simon.

"This is my best friend," said Melissa. "I'd trust her with my life."

"τεο ύολς φί νναα υ εε απ νακαέ," said Jillian. ("Don't push your luck I haven't eaten for days.")

Simon and Ross released Jillian. She flapped her wings in an attempt to get off her back—but failed. The boys gently rolled her over. She sat up and preened her pink feathers with her ugly crooked beak.

"Right," said Melissa. "Jillian will fly us, one by one, to the top of the castle."

"Ross can go first," said Simon.

"Why me?" asked Ross.

"Because you're my best friend," said Simon, slapping Ross on the back.

"Thanks," replied Ross, not really understanding why this meant he should go first.

He scrambled onto Jillian's back, wrapping his arms around her neck as tightly as he could without actually strangling her. Jillian ran along the ground flapping her wings. Eventually she rose into the air. Then she fell towards the ground. Then she rose into the air again. Narrowly missing several trees she flew in a zig-zag-ooops sort of way towards the castle. With all the finesse of a mad bull in a burger bar she crash landed onto the castle turret. Ross jumped off—surprised to still be alive. Two more precarious flights later all three were perched on the roof.

"Thanks for your help," said Melissa. "If we survive our visit to the castle I'll see you soon."

"Δίταια της έτης δίατια," said Jillian. ("Yeah, but only if my back isn't broken from carrying your weight.")

CHAPTER 36
Melissa gets a big fright from a little monster

From the top of the castle the children had a clear view down the mountainside to the village and the shoreline beyond. Stretched out before them lay the full extent of Doctor X's scigic; mythical creatures everywhere—on the ground and in the air. Not only had all the villagers been transformed but, minute by minute, more wild animals and farm animals were changing into strange, dangerous beasts.

"Well this is it," said Simon solemnly. "If we can't beat Doctor X we'll soon be ugly monsters too."

"Speak for yourself," said Melissa sulkily.

"Sorry," said Simon. "I didn't mean to insult you and anyway your snakes are actually quite nice."

Melissa smiled. Her snakes stopped spitting at Simon.

"By the looks of it Doctor X must be about finished here. If we can't stop him he'll soon move to the mainland," said Simon.

"And after that the whole world will be filled with his beasts," said Ross.

"Well, before we risk our lives again there's one thing I need to know," said Simon.

"What's that?" asked Ross.

"Something that's been annoying me for days," said Simon. "What's the answer to your riddle?"

"Are you sure we've got time for me to explain?" asked Ross. Simon looked at his Ultra-Accurate-Atomic-Wrist-Watch. He took it off, stared at it for a few seconds then threw it over the castle parapet. The Ultra-Accurate-Atomic-Wrist-Watch tumbled down, narrowly missed Argos, and hit the stone path. It smashed into one-hundred pieces.

"We've got all the time you want," said Simon.

"The answer is six moves," said Ross. "I'm afraid I cheated a bit—it's a trick question. The pawn doesn't actually return as a pawn. It becomes a queen and then return to its own square—so I didn't actually tell a lie."

As Simon only knew half the rules of chess and those that he half knew were half wrong it took Ross a full ten minutes to explain the solution. He explained how the pieces moved and about queening a pawn and in passing he even explained the enpassant rule. Finally Simon was satisfied that he understood the riddle.

"Okay," he said, patting Ross and Melissa on their backs. "Let's get Doctor X."

With the help of a drainpipe they scrambled from the roof onto a window ledge on the top floor of the castle. They peered inside. The room was completely empty. Simon took off a shoe, smashed a small window and they clambered inside. Quietly they crossed the room and opened a door that led them to a long corridor. It was dark and eerie and if they hadn't been so terrified of meeting Doctor X they would have been terrified of meeting a ghost. Dozens of rooms led off from the corridor. As they went along, they opened each door cautiously but every room was completely empty—except one. At the far end of the corridor they found Doctor X's bedroom. Simon went in first. When he was sure it was safe, he beckoned to Ross and Melissa.

The room was large and lit by just two candles. It was sparsely furnished—at the far side under the curtained window was Doctor X's bed and scattered around the room were a few old tables and cabinets. The walls were covered in cuttings from scientific magazines—most of them about Doctor X's failed experiments or articles criticizing his many attempts to make mythical creatures. But Doctor X had crossed out and changed words so that all the articles praised him. One which originally said, "Doctor X is the dumbest scientist in the world," now read "Doctor X is the ~~dumb~~best scientist in the world." Another which once said, "Doctor X is a useless idiot—his silly experiments are all doomed to fail," had also been modified by Doctor X—but I'll leave you to work out what he'd changed that to.

The twitching candles cast eerie shadows against the walls. Fear crept under Melissa's skin, growing rapidly until it became unbearable. She quivered like an elephant unexpectedly caught in an Arctic blizzard.

"This place spooks me," she hissed, "let's get out of here."

"Just another few minutes," insisted Simon.

Melissa stayed close to the door as the boys explored the room. They were all suddenly startled by a creepy creaking noise coming from the far corner. Melissa fought back the urge to scream. Cautiously the boys edged towards the corner. As well as the creaking there was now also a quieter squeaking. Ross got there first.

"It's only a mouse," he said, "or mice."

Melissa screamed—she hated mice.

There, on a table, was a small cage. Inside was a wheel with a mouse frantically trying to make it turn. The mouse had two heads—one at either end of its body. One half was trying to run one way while the other half struggled to go in the opposite direction. As a result the wheel rocked back and forward creating the eerie creaking. On the cage was a little plaque which read, "The first ever mythical creature to be created by the World Famous and Exceptionally Important Scientist Doctor X".

"Let's go," said Simon. "There's nothing here that can help us."

"Except these," he added, grabbing two large silver candlesticks and thrusting one into Ross's hands. "These will make great weapons."

They left the room and headed down the stairway to the ground floor.

A ferocious roar erupted from the darkness. Cerberus launched his attack.

CHAPTER 37
Melissa tries to teach a three headed dog new tricks

Cerberus was Doctor X's favorite creation. In ancient times he'd guarded the underworld, not to stop anyone getting in, no his job was to make sure that the dead never escaped back to the land of the living. Cerberus looked like a bloodthirsty pit-bull terrier except that he was eight times larger, had a long dragon-like tail and three savage heads. He was a thug of a dog. A bit like the typical school bully, he had very little brain in his heads but what he lacked in intelligence he made up for in aggression. Cerberus had loved his job—okay, so he had to work an eternity of hours, but it provided him with an endless supply of food—for when anyone tried sneaking passed him he would rip them apart juicy bone by juicy bone.

Cerberus was dreaming about skeletons when he was rudely awaken by the children rushing down the stairs. He believed that he was still guarding the underworld. He thought the children were trying to escape from the eternal damnation of hell. It was his duty to stop them. It was his greatest desire to destroy them slowly and painfully. He sprung into action. Saliva spraying from his mouths, he leapt the stairs nine at a time.

"This way," yelled Simon, taking a left at the foot of the stairs. Ross followed but Melissa had fallen behind. As she reached the last few stairs Cerberus bounded past. Growling and snarling, he turned to face her. Melissa tried the tricks you should usually try when confronted by a killer three-headed dog. In her friendliest voice she said, "who's a good doggy," and "nice puppy lie down and I'll tickle your tummy." But it was no use——Cerberus had already set his heart on playing jigsaw with her bones.

Slowly Melissa backed up the stairs again. Step by step Cerberus followed her——shepherding her up to his 'underworld' and a torturous death.

CHAPTER 38
Simon and Ross see the funny side of Doctor X's experiments

Simon and Ross fled along the dark corridor unaware that Melissa had been left behind and was in danger of becoming a doggy treat. They burst into a room marked, 'Doctor X's Top Secret Laboratory. Do not enter or ELSE!'.

Sitting at the far end of the room, was Doctor X, so absorbed in his books that he didn't notice them charging in.

"Quick. Under the table," whispered Simon.

The boys crawled under, out of sight of Doctor X.

"Where's Melissa?" asked Ross.

"Dunno," said Simon.

"We'd better look for her," said Ross.

"She'll be okay," said Simon. "She'll have escaped into another room."

"But that dog . . ." said Ross.

"Melissa can take care of herself," said Simon, "We'll take care of Doctor X."

"But Melissa thinks she can persuade . . ." said Ross.

"We do this my way," interrupted Simon abruptly.

"Your way?" said Ross.

"Our way," said Simon. "Our way is better than persuasion."

"I don't think that's fair," said Ross.

"Looking for Melissa is too risky," said Simon. "We need to do this now. Come on."

Candlesticks raised above their heads, the boys tiptoed towards the evil scientist. At the precise moment they reached his desk Doctor X completed a long complex formula. This gave him a more effective way of modifying DNA. With this new formula a tiny drop carried by the wind would transform millions of people in a matter of hours.

"Eureeeeeekaaa!!!!" he yelled, jumping to his feet. "Sooner than soon I will rule the world. Ha ha he he he."

"Not if we can help it," said Simon, shaking so much he was in danger of hitting his own head with the candlestick.

"And who are you?" asked Doctor X calmly.

"I'm Simon Fairleywelthy of 42 Burn Road, Invermorethan and this is my best friend Ross McBagpipe. We're twelve years old and we go to Invermorethan School," said Simon, which was really too formal an introduction considering the circumstances.

"What are you doing in my top secret laboratory?" asked Doctor X in the sort of evil voice you'd expect from a mad scientist.

"Stopping you turning people into horrible monsters," said Simon, thrusting the silver candlestick towards Doctor X.

"That's right," said Ross as an added threat.

"Ha ha ha he he," laughed Doctor X. "And how do you propose to stop me?"

"We'll kill you if necessary," said Simon in the bravest, deepest, most threatening voice he could muster while trying to stop his knees from knocking together.

"Yeah," added Ross. "And if that doesn't work we'll torture you."

"I think torturing would probably need to be before killing," said Simon.

"I don't think killing is such a good idea," said Ross.

"But we might have to," insisted Simon.

"Well, can we try torture first?" said Ross.

"Okay," said Simon. "But if he doesn't do as we say . . ."

"Not killing and torture. I hate violence," said Doctor X, sounding more like a gentle old man than the mad scientist he really was.

"We'll do whatever we have to do to stop your evil plan," said Simon growing in courage.

"In that case I surrender," said Doctor X. "I give up my plan to rule the world."

"Good," said Simon. "Now turn everyone back to normal please."

"Okay," said Doctor X, "but put those candlesticks down first."

"No way," said Simon.

"I'm not turning anyone back until you put the candlesticks down," said Doctor X.

"Turn them back first," insisted Simon, "then we'll put the candlesticks down."

"No! You first!" said Doctor X.

"No! You first!" said Simon.

"No!" said Simon.

"Double No!" said Doctor X.

"Triple No!" said Simon.

"No! No! No! No!" exclaimed Doctor X thumping his desk.

"It's not that we don't trust you," said Ross. "It's just that . . ."

"You're like all the others," snapped Doctor X. "You think I'm insane."

"No, we think you're extremely clever," said Ross. "But in an evil, cruel, spiteful, uncaring, selfish sort of way."

"Selfish! Me! Never!" exclaimed Doctor X.

Grabbing a small phial from his desk he yelled, "Here's a present to show how kind I can be."

Before the boys could react, Doctor X threw the contents of the phial at them. As it hit their faces the liquid turned to gas.

Immediately they started laughing uncontrollably.

"So you think laughing gas is a laughing matter," sneered Doctor X.

"That's really funny," chuckled Simon, tears of laughter streaming down his face.

"Laughing gas a laughing matter," giggled Ross. "What a silly thing to say."

"Nothing I do is silly," bellowed Doctor X. "I am the greatest scientist in the whole world, probably the whole universe."

"Why did the mad scientist take over the world?" asked Simon roaring with laughter.

"I don't know," said Ross. "Why did the mad scientist take over the world?"

"To get to the other side," giggled Simon, rolling about on the floor.

"No," exclaimed Ross hysterically. "The joke is 'why did the chicken take over the world?'"

"Or maybe it's 'why did the mad scientist cross the road?'" corrected Simon.

"And now my little friends, you will help me with an experiment," said Doctor X. "I will turn you both into winged horses. You will be called Pegasus-One and Pegasus-Two and you will fly me from country to country so that in a matter of days every continent will be under my control . . . ha ha he he he."

"Let me be Pegasus-One," sniggered Ross.

"No. Me. Me. Me," laughed Simon punching Ross in the face. "I want to be Pegasus-One."

"No way," sniggered Ross, kicking his friend, "I'm going to be Pegasus-One."

"Over my dead body," sniggered Simon.

While the boys fought, Doctor X took a beaker of yellow liquid from his desk. Stirring in the heart of a poisonous dart toad and the crushed bodies of twelve cockroaches he chanted,

Heart plucked from toad with a magical spell,
Mixed up with stuff too gruesome to tell,
Bring from the past the most evil of forces,
To turn horrid boys into nice flying horses.

Carefully he poured the liquid into two small glasses.

"Drink this!" he commanded.

Simon and Ross took the glasses.

"I've never tasted juice made from the heart of a toad," laughed Simon. "Is it better than cola?"

"Drink!" yelled Doctor X.

"You first," sniggered Ross.

"No you go first," said Simon, laughing so hard that some of the liquid splashed onto his jeans.

"What's that really funny barking noise?" asked Ross.

"It's must be that cute three headed doggy," laughed Simon. "That will be Melissa coming to rescue us."

"No. She'll be a pile of chewed up bones by now," chuckled Ross.

"Ha ha ha," laughed Simon. "I hope it didn't eat her funny bone."

"Thanks for warning me that you have another nasty little friend," sneered Doctor X.

CHAPTER 39
Doctor X gets a taste of his own medicine

octor X reached the door just as Melissa slammed it shut. On the other side Cerberus snarled and growled as he mauled the door with bone-shredding claws.

"Welcome back my pretty little Medusa," sneered Doctor X, grabbing Melissa from behind. "Now you can watch your interfering little friends as I alter their DNA forever."

Melissa struggled to escape from Doctor X's clutches.

"Let me go you monster," she yelled.

"Oh that's rich," snarled Doctor X. "The girl with snakes in her hair calling me a monster."

Melissa stamped with all her might on Doctor X's feet.

"You little brat," he yelled, as Melissa slipped from his grasp. Melissa grabbed one of the candlesticks and swung round to hit Doctor X.

"Don't you dare ..." Doctor X began to scream. But his words froze in the air.

"Ha. Ha," roared Ross. "Look, the mad scientist has turned to stone."

"Now he's a mad statue not a mad scientist," chuckled Simon.

"Mad," laughed Ross, "He certainly doesn't look too happy with Melissa."

"It's not funny," snapped Melissa. "Now we can't make him reverse the scigic."

"Oh excuse me for breathing," laughed Ross putting the glass to his lips. "Well you're not getting any of my nice juice—so there."

"Don't drink that," screamed Melissa.

"Will so," said Ross.

Melissa dived across the room. She swung the candlestick and knocked the glass from Ross's hands. The liquid cascaded down his clothes.

"That wasn't very nice," giggled Ross.

"Not getting mine," sniggered Simon.

Melissa whacked the candlestick down on Simon's arm.

"Boo hoo, you hurt my arm," tittered Simon, "and made me drop my juice."

"This isn't funny," cried Melissa. "Come on I need your help."

"No, what you need is a hairdresser," laughed Simon.

"Or a zoo keeper," giggled Ross.

"Stop being silly," said Melissa. "That beast of a dog is breaking down the door. We're trapped in here."

"Who cares?" laughed Simon. "His bark is probably worse than his bite."

"You mean his three barks are probably worse than his three bites," sniggered Ross.

"Can you please be serious," snapped Melissa. "We've only got minutes to find a way to reverse the scigic."

"Maybe there's an antidote amongst Doctor X's notes," laughed Ross.

The laughing gas was gradually wearing off and the boys were beginning to think sensibly again.

"Great idea," said Melissa.

Melissa grabbed the Experiment Book and flicked through it. All it contained was formulae for creating creatures not for uncreating them. Cerberus had now ripped a large hole in the door. He squeezed his heads through. Saliva dripping from his mouths he scowled at the children then continued the demolition.

"Hurry up," yelled Simon. "Check the index."

Melissa turned to the back of the book. Another chunk of door crashed to the floor.

"Creating Cyclopes . . . DNA Designs for Dragons . . . Genetically Generating Giants . . . Making Medusas . . . Ten Things to Do With Chicken . . ." lilted Melissa reading down the list of contents. "There's nothing about reversing the scigic."

"There must be something," said Simon.

"Unless there is no way to reverse it," said Ross.

"If only I hadn't turned Doctor X to stone . . ." said Melissa.

"Yeah," said Simon. "We'd all be monsters by now."

Pushing with his massive body, Cerberus smashed down the rest of the door and burst through. Snarling through bone crunching teeth he charged at the children. There was nowhere to run, nowhere to hide. This was the bit that made Cerberus's job worthwhile. Killing was his greatest love. He'd spent his whole life tormenting the dead—but even if that hadn't been part of his job he'd still have done it just for fun. All of his eyes were fixed on his victims. He saw the despair in their faces. He smelt their fear—a kind of fear that he'd never smelt before. Their fear was not selfish but a fear that was for each other and for mankind. He almost felt sorry for them—but he didn't. He loathed their pathetic sentimentality. He would show them no mercy.

"Catch," cried Melissa, as instinctively she threw the Experiment Book at the heartless beast.

With all three sets of savage teeth Cerberus attacked the book. Tearing and slashing at its pages he hacked it to bits. Melissa had hoped to distract Cerberus long enough for them to escape but it was no use, within seconds he'd shredded the book and devoured the pieces. The book was gone and with it all of Doctor X's secrets. With a crazed glare in his eyes, Cerberus leapt. Simon and Ross threw themselves out of his way. Melissa tried to escape but the weight of the beast bore down upon her. Sharp claws sank into her stomach as she was thrown to the floor.

"Get those candlesticks," yelled Simon.

Held down by the brute's great weight Melissa stared into its eyes begging for mercy. It gorged on her fear, feasting on the terror that oozed from her every pore.

"Catch," shrieked Ross, throwing a candlestick to Simon.

With blood-red tongues Cerberus licked its three savage sets of teeth. The very last scrap of the Experiment Book dislodged from a tooth. In a final display of malice Cerberus made a great show of devouring this morsel.

Weapons in hand the boys dived at the beast, smashing the candlesticks down on its massive back. They bounced off. Cerberus didn't even notice. He gave a haunting howl then thrust forward to snap off Melissa's head.

Melissa screamed. She closed her eyes, ready to meet her end. But there was no agonizing pain—no torturous ripping of flesh—no decapitation.

She opened her eyes. She let out an even louder scream.

"Aaaaaaagggggghhhhh, get this mouse off my nose."

The terrified mouse scurried away across the floor.

"The beast . . . ," yelled Ross in disbelief, " . . . it turned into a mouse,"

"And your snakes have gone Melissa," screeched Simon. "You look almost normal."

Melissa pulled herself up off the floor and ran her fingers through her hair.

"You know what this means," she said.

"That you can use a hairbrush again?" said Simon.

"No," replied Melissa. "Destroying Doctor X's Experiment Book has destroyed all his scigic."

Melissa was right—at least partly right. The unique combination of Doctor X being turned to stone by the Medusa he had created and his Experiment Book being devoured by one of his own mythical creatures was the one and only way to reverse his scigic. Instantly the villagers and animals turned back to normal. Many of them got rather a shock!

Farmer Ben Cattlegrid who had been turned into a Nine-Headed-Hydra suddenly found himself in a muddy swamp wearing only his thermal underwear and had to rush home before anyone spotted him. He decided to keep the stone collection that he'd gathered. It took six weeks to transport them all by tractor to his farm. It's now the biggest collection of stones on Gogha and Ben is shortly opening a Stone Museum.

The three friends Elizabeth, Hannah and Alice who had been turned into ugly Harpies were at the top of a rather tall tree when their scigic was reversed. Not until the following day were they discovered and rescued by the island's only fire engine. The girls still argue about which of them was the ugliest.

On the mainland the children that Melissa had turned to stone all returned to normal. The weird magic that caused everyone to forget them had also been destroyed. Suddenly everyone forgot that they had forgotten them. Their images on photos and their names on documents all reappeared. Even though Chris has met Melissa a number of times since she turned him to stone he still avoids looking her in the eyes—just in case. Ann Dromeda was so impressed with Simon's unselfish bravery that she agreed to go to the movies with him and they have gone to a movie every day since.

Melissa's cat, Snowy, now has the tendency to dance rather than to walk in normal cat-like manner. This has made mouse hunting almost impossible but Snowy doesn't seem to mind. She is no longer able to talk, but Melissa is sure that she understands every word she hears.

And so everyone and everything on Gogha and the mainland returned to normal. What is surprising is that none of the islanders killed or ate each other while they were vicious creatures, but that was just a matter of good fortune. Actually when I say, 'everyone and everything returned to normal' that is not completely true. What I should have said was 'everyone and everything returned to normal—except Doctor X.' Because he was so wickedly evil, the magic powers that turned him to stone did not reverse. Doctor X never, ever returned to his normal self.

CHAPTER 40
Everyone lives happily ever after-well almost everyone

T wo weeks after Simon, Ross and Melissa had saved the world they were invited to a celebration at Lochlinda Village Square. The whole island turned out along with many people from the mainland. Mrs. Wanabea Fairleywelthy's pink-leather sofa was specially flown over—strapped to the rotor blades of a helicopter. Despite being rather dizzy, Mrs. Fairleywelthy remained on her pink-leather sofa during the flight so she could watch her portable televisions. Mr. Fairleywelthy looked very respectable wearing his black Mafia Hit Man double breasted suit complete with Beretta 92SD pistol-with-silencer and color coordinated Heckler Koch MP-5 submachine gun. Ross's parents were there too of course. His mom used up thirty-seven boxes of paper hankies during the ceremony and completely soaked Mrs. Fairleywelthy's pink-leather sofa with her tears.

The Chief of Police opened the ceremony. He began, "It is a shocking sign of how disobedient our youth have become that we are here today to hang three children for attempting to take over the world."

Mayor Mainotte, the Mayor of Gogha, nudged the Chief and reminded him that the children had in fact saved the world.

"Ahhhmm, sorry about that mix up," continued the Chief. "It is very grudgingly that I must thank these almost-quite-nice children Melissa, Ross and What's-His-Name for saving the world from the evil Doctor X. But I must warn them that if they ever do so again, without first getting permission in triplicate from the Council they will be locked up in a cold, dark prison cell with only a slice of dry bread on alternate Wednesdays . . . "

An hour later, when the Chief of Police had finally finished his speech, the children were each presented with a bravery award. Melissa's was a golden hair dryer, Ross got a gold and silver chess set and Simon was given an Extra-Ultra-Exceedingly-Accurate-Atomic-Wrist-Watch.

"There's just one thing left to do," said Mayor Mainotte, "and that is to unveil this monument to commemorate the bravery of these special children."

The crowd fell silent and eagerly shuffled forward. The Mayor's wife pulled a silk ribbon and a large sheet cascaded to the ground revealing a wonderful statue. From the little wart on the tip of its nose to the crooked black cane in its right hand it was perfect in every detail.

In unison the crowd gasped, "Wow".

Mrs. Fairleywelthy fell off her pink-leather sofa.

Simon nudged Ross in the ribs.

"Your girlfriend makes really cool statues—don't forget to wear your sunglasses when you're with her."

Ross and Melissa both kicked Simon.

The monument that would forever grace the village square was the stone statue of Doctor X.

Inscribed on a plaque attached to his bottom were the words, "This statue is a reminder to all evil scientists that the use of science for selfish, greedy purposes is very, very naughty indeed."